CW01202448

MOBIUS BLVD

Stories from the Byway Between Reality and Dream

JUNE | 2024

No. 8

CONTENTS

A HERO FOR HIS PEOPLE

Jason Lairamore

Darkness was complete, but there was heat, and it moved in ways it shouldn't, in silent rushes first this way then that, like the chugging of some great beast breathing out over the surface of this far-flung rock of a planetoid.

Heat was how Moatvey always found Kayrill. Kayrill should have figured that out by now, but, as luck would have it, he hadn't, and that was fine by Moatvey. He was his people's rightful hero, after all.

He saw Kayrill's cloaked harvester fine through his specs even on a world as black as this. It sat there, just as happy as it pleased, collecting ore as fast as it could, as if it didn't realize it was poaching on a planet surrounded by monstrous aliens that would pick it apart if they ever found it.

After a quick perimeter check, he jumped to the harvester's port and scurried inside. He made sure to check for traps as he went. Kayrill had left snares and the like at the last few ore collectors he had stolen.

This one looked clean. He made his quick way to the control access patch.

The command panel was lit up with flashing warning lights.

His hearts ran a mismatched cadence. The giant aliens had pinged the harvester. They were on their way. He rolled his head to cover the 360 then pecked away simultaneously on the console's three boards. The harvesters were designed to flee if detected, to get off planet and head home, but this one wasn't. Something was wrong.

Then he found it. Kayrill had rigged the collector to fail.

As he punched the three boards to work a bypass and get the machine moving, he picked up a comm from the approaching aliens.

"Something is making that vibration," one said.

"Yes, yes, something surely is," said another. "I'm just saying it is not little green men."

The laughter that followed sent a shiver down Moatvey's spine. Every time the giant aliens saw anything out of the ordinary they started jabbering about 'little green men'. It was like they somehow knew about Moatvey and his people even though none of them had ever actually seen one of Moatvey's kin. The fact they seemed to know what he looked like was terrifying. It was like they had some kind of biological super-sense that he and his people had yet to discover.

He got around the harvester's artificial intel and punched up the escape vectors manually. It'd be a slow trip back home, the poaching machines were built to make as few waves as possible, but at least he would get away.

Damn that devious Kayrill. He would pay for this.

Kayrill. He and Moatvey had been friends once. They had even been chosen as the pair to go out on the seven year mission to see if they could catch an errant asteroid for mining. Back then, their people had been so low on resources.

That mission had been such a success. They had managed to land on the asteroid, but they hadn't been alone. An unmanned scout ship from the aliens had found it first.

It had been their people's greatest scientific discovery. The alien ship had an interstellar drive, something their people still hadn't been able to reproduce.

Since then, he and Kayrill had managed to steal twelve other interstellar engines. They had been ghosting the giant aliens ever since in hopes of stealing more.

That Kayrill had set the harvester to get caught was insane. It had to be more than mere revenge against Moatvey for his stealing away the precious ships for his own gain. Why, the aliens could have found the unit, and then they might have discovered the existence of their people.

Something unthinkable was brewing inside Kayrill's befuddled mind. Kayrill knew, just as Moatvey knew, what those alien monsters were capable of doing. He had seen their wasteful atrocities and beast-like behavior just as often as Moatvey.

There would be problems by the time he reached home. He just knew it.

The harvester hit atmosphere, and Moatvey was ready. If Kayrill had gone crazy, then he probably had some kind of crazy plan. The best way to counter that was to be unpredictable.

So he would do the craziest thing he could think to do.

He would fight crazy with crazy.

He ran to the interstellar engine and wedged his vice pliers into the casing surrounding its core then took off at a jolting lope to the impact cocoon he'd rigged up. He slid into its narrow hole and pulled the cork in after him.

The harvester's interstellar engine blew up, and he was plastered against the spongy cocoon walls. Free-fall followed then impact. He bounced for a time before stopping.

He exited to the sound of screams, but didn't waste time to examine the damage he had caused. He ran away. Nobody paid him any mind. Everybody was headed toward the devastation.

But not him. He ran toward the greater need. His people needed a hero.

Kayrill had to be stopped.

Everything everywhere was white circular domiciles. In many places they were stacked over twenty high. And in between the great white balls were white plastic strollways. Every so often there was a different color ball indicating a store, or a workplace. He found a locater box and checked where he was.

Zeneta. She was Kayrill's most favorite ex-wife, though he doubted that she knew it. Kayrill still loved her. She was the one person that Kayrill cherished above all others. He found where her domicile was and hopped a transport.

He kicked open the door of her home and entered in a rush. She lay back at her ease watching the news vids of the accident he had caused. He could hear the Newsman speak of it as he spun toward her. Her eyes were brimmed full of tears at the news. He wondered, briefly, how bad it had been but clamped down on the guilty supposition. He could grieve later, after he made sure that the whole of his people were safe.

Her tears fell as she blinked at his sudden, noisy appearance.

"Moatvey?" she asked, bringing one of her arms up toward her face.

He jumped to her and had her bound before she could ask him what was going on.

"Kayrill has to be stopped," he said. The dark light in her eyes brightened with the mention of that name.

"But --," she began.

"Later," he commanded. "It's not safe here." He dragged her away from the vidscreen and shuffled to her private transport. Once he had her secure, he revved up the transport's engine and entered the main thoroughfare.

He needed some distance from her residence. Kayrill might have guessed that he would get to Zeneta. In any event, he now had a bargaining platform by which to deal.

"Moatvey, I'm frightened," she said from the seat next to him.

He responded softly. It wasn't her fault that Kayrill had gone insane.

"Don't worry," he said. "All I need you to do is call Kayrill."

"What's he done? She asked. "Was he responsible for that crash this morning?" She shook her head before continuing. "I always knew he'd get too involved, that he'd go too far. He never had your level head Moatvey. Your friendship over the years had always kept him steady. Since you two had gone your separate ways I've done nothing but worry."

"You and me both," he replied.

He pointed to the communicator hooked to the front panel of the transport.

"Contact him. Tell him you're with me."

She grabbed the device and paused. "I don't know his information."

"It hasn't changed," he said. It hadn't changed because Kayrill had wanted to leave a way for Zeneta to contact him if she ever felt the need. Moatvey was tempted to tell her this but held back. She had enough on her mind already.

While she made her connection he entered the coordinates to one of his secret storage facilities into the transport.

"Kayrill," she said. "Is that you?"

"Tell him who you are with," he said.

She did.

"Now end the contact."

She did so without hesitation.

"What's going on?" she asked.

He shook his head. "I'll tell you after, I promise."

They arrived at his secret storage building and took off in an interstellar moments later.

"Call him back," he told her, handing her the communicator.

They were in high orbit above the planet with the planet's communication satellites well within range of his devices.

She punched in Kayrill's number. He handed her a piece of parchment with a star location grid-set written neatly upon it.

"Tell him to meet us there," he said.

She nodded. "When?"

"Now." He fiddled with his ship's controls as she waited for Kayrill.

"Kayrill," she said into the communicator. "Yes, I'm fine. No, he hasn't hurt me." She looked over at Moatvey. "No, he doesn't want to talk to you." She read off the grid-set. "Meet us there."

"Cease the call," Moatvey said. She did.

“What's going on?"

"We're going to a comet," he said, "a fast moving one, with a very low albedo. It is real hard to see. The perfect place."

"A comet," she repeated, looking out the window. Moatvey sometimes forgot that the masses were so less travelled than he and Kayrill.

The interstellar was quiet as he readied it for the burn to the comet. He glanced over at Zeneta a time or two, but she continued to look out the window toward the world below.

"Ready?" he asked.

She nodded, still looking away. "He called you a coward. It was the last thing I heard before cutting the connection."

"I don't care what he said," he replied and hit the ignition to the interstellar drive.

The surface of the comet was broken, black rock spotted here and there with white out-gassings. He launched his detection drones then suited up. He had Zeneta do the same before they headed outside.

Kayrill stepped out from behind a rocky outcropping as soon as he and Zeneta were a dozen hops from the ship.

"What have you done Kayrill?" Zeneta asked before either Moatvey or Kayrill could say anything.

Kayrill gave her a big smile. Moatvey frowned. That smile was too predatory. It reminded him of the aliens.

"I'm glad you are here to witness my crowning achievement Zeneta," Kayrill said.

"You're not achieving anything," Moatvey said, grabbing Zeneta. He pulled a blade from his pocket and put its edge against her throat.

Kayrill didn't seem the least bit perturbed. "If you had put a knife to her before that explosion you caused I'd not have taken you seriously. Now though, I'm willing to bet that you'd actually do it. You've learned a thing or two from our large friends it seems."

Zeneta began to tremble in his grasp. Kayrill shook his head. Moatvey didn't like how he continued to remain so calm.

"We both know why you brought me here," Kayrill said.

Moatvey paused. He had been delaying, had been dragging out the inevitable, just to make sure that Kayrill hadn't any more tricks to pull. That Kayrill was acting so pleased with himself was unnerving.

"You're right," he said. There had been enough talk. It was time to end this. His people needed him. He was their hero. And Kayrill was in the way.

He bent and whispered into Zeneta's ear, "You want to know what is going on?" he asked. "I'm going to kill you. Then I am going to kill Kayrill."

He tightened his grip on the knife and made ready to use it against her trembling form.

"There can only be one hero," he said, loud enough for Kayrill to hear.

One of his detector drones dinged. He jerked to check the panel on his wrist and Zeneta wrenched herself away. She bounded toward Kayrill. He made to follow but saw what was standing behind the still smiling Kayrill.

Two giant monster aliens were there. One had a gun pointed at him.

"They were here the entire time," Kayrill said, "behind the same rock as I." He turned to Zeneta who was about halfway between the two. "I told them to make sure no harm came to you. You were never in any danger Zeneta."

She just stared at him then at Moatvey then at the aliens.

"You really are crazy!" Moatvey moaned. There stood two members of the most wretched species ever conceived. "You've seen their histories! You know what they have done!"

Kayrill turned to the two giants. "I've been trying to capture him for months. His behavior has been on a steady decline since the contact between our races. He set off an explosion that killed over a hundred of my kind a short time ago. And you saw what he was ready to do to dear Zeneta. As you can see, what I told you is true."

What had Kayrill been telling them? Why had he been talking to them at all? They were monsters.

"What have you done?" he asked. "You have doomed us all."

Kayrill shook his head. "We are overpopulated and without resources. We must have their interstellar tech. There are things we have that they do not. Mutual trade between us and them can and will be achieved."

Moatvey just stared. The monsters were smiling at him. He could see their hard teeth from here, teeth for ripping and tearing, teeth for masticating. They were beasts. What guarantee did they have that the aliens wouldn't simply come and kill his entire race, or enslave them, or simply take anything they wanted and then be on their merry way. He'd seen their history. They were more than capable of doing any of those atrocious things.

"Your days of villainous greed and monopolizing the situation are at an end," Kayrill continued. "It is not up to you to single handedly control the handful of interstellar we have. Our people have a right to know. They need to know everything."

Moatvey dropped the knife he had been carrying. The alien that had the gun pointed at him didn't drop its weapon.

They all just looked at him, as if waiting for him to say something in his defense. He could have said that he'd been doing what he was doing because he was trying to protect his people from a bigger, more aggressive species, that all he wanted to do was try to keep the two cultures apart until his people were stronger. But, he didn't say anything like that. It was too late now. Kayrill had seen to that.

Kayrill looked once again to the monsters. "Our kind isn't ready to associate too directly with your culture, as Moatvey here proves. Relations must be slow."

"We can respect that," one of the monsters said.

'Could they?' Moatvey wondered. Were they even capable of understanding the notion of respect?

"If you have a need to rid yourself of this one," the monster that had spoken before continued, "perhaps you could release him into our care. Maybe we could learn more about each other through a dialog with him?"

Kayrill looked to the hard black rock at his feet.

"I'll go," Moatvey said. The alternative was to be removed from the situation, to be put on trial and probably sent to prison.

Kayrill nodded and one of the giants approached.

So the monsters were coming. At least he would be there to witness it. And, who knew, perhaps, one day, he could find a way to be of some service, just in case his people needed him.

They might, still yet, need a hero.

EYE OF THE BEHOLDER

TS S. Fulk

The ground shook with each thunderous footfall the new gods took. We cowered in the basement of an abandoned schoolhouse. Every step sprinkled ceiling plaster dust on us like sugar on a monk's doughnut.

Time stretched, and sweat burned our eyes. Ignoring the sweat, Jolleen's eyes darted back and forth like she was high on perc. Her muscles tensed on the edge of a foolhardy dash.

"Not yet!" a harsh whisper rebuked. Maia took command easily, as was her nature. "Count to 500. Sign when you're done. Once we're out. Don't look back at them."

I counted in my head, both eyes fixed on Joleen. Her face was concentrating on numbers, and her muscles relaxed. Too soon, she gave a thumbs up. I had only reached 392 myself.

Maia raised her left hand, palm flat, and held it in suspended animation. My own muscles readied to run. The instant the open palm became a fist, we were off. Joleen practically flew up the stairs silently taking two steps a leap. Maia followed, and I brought up the rear.

Once out of the school, we dashed building to building, behind where a new god strode. Before getting the correct angle to keep the thing behind me, curiosity got the better of me, so I stole a peek. It towered above the decrepit buildings. My eyes, or maybe my brain, couldn't focus properly on it— it's bulk covered by a shimmering iridescent black smoke.

My heart skipped a beat, and my mind froze, only for a few seconds. I stumbled, not too loudly, jolting my head out of that black shimmering fog. Yet, the damage was done, and I had damned my friends with that selfish glance, for I felt inky tendrils entering my brain.

We were halfway home. Each with scavenged medicine and supplies in our backpacks. We branched off into separate alleys. The god must have turned around, for it's thunder steps grew louder. I concentrated with running straight and fast—my duty. Joleen and Maia would dart and turn in complex patterns, eventually to dash home.

A few minutes later, I heard Joleen howl an inhuman cry, as if her spirit was being stripped from her flesh. I blocked it out, urging my feet to accelerate. The howls echoed off the buildings for at least ten minutes.

In the silence that followed, I tried to ignore the burning of my lungs, the ache in my knees and the hole in my heart—tears adding their salt to the sweat on my face. I ran straight ahead. I did my duty.

I arrived at the old mines, which was our underground camp and promptly collapsed. Justine, one of our healalls, took my pack and helped me to a bed. Ten minutes later, Maia stumbled in. "You've doomed us," she cried, hands on knees, gasping between words.

"What?"

"It'll follow you now. Go! Get out of here fast!" She then shook off Justine's help and ordered the immediate evacuation of the camp. Turning to me, as I was struggled to get up, she spat, "You're cursed now. Go and lead the thing away. Then stay far away from us."

The guards lifted me to my feet and started pushing me out. I tried to say something in protest, but was too drained to do anything except sob quietly as I stubbled out of the entrance. A growing thunder rained in the distance.

I started to realize what I had done and walked as quickly away as my fatigued muscles allowed. But it was too late. The thunder had reached the mines. I held my hands over my ears to block out the howling shrieks that were to come.

Now I roam the wastelands. My pet god following on its leash.

HEINRICH AND THE WITCH

Pete Barnstrom

The stories said that the old woman was a witch.

She lured children into her cottage, they said, and boiled them in a pot, by which she could then distill their youth into a potion or tincture, or perhaps an invigorating ointment. That's why she was so old, the stories said, she'd lived forever on the essence of children.

They also said that she could command the weather, bend the beasts and insects to her will, and that she had hands in the form of chicken feet. The stories were vague as to the utility of this final skill, but it was evil.

The witch's power, the stories said, was incalculable, and its origin infernal.

Magic. Black magic.

As a twelve-year-old man of science, Heinrich did not believe in magic, nor witches, and one fine morning he determined to set off and have his proof.

He donned his most courageous lederhosen and his sturdiest hiking boots. He collected a few supplies from his laboratory into his rucksack.

Heinrich left early in the day, as he was not entirely sure where the witch's cottage was, and he wanted to be home in time for supper, having smelled baking strudel in Oma's kitchen. Oh, how Heinrich loved his Oma's strudel.

He entered his forest.

It was a nice one, his forest, shady and thick with animals, but trees sufficiently spaced so that he was able to maintain a steady pace. He spied a hedgehog burrow and, when he peeked inside, the back of a pale, prickly coat. A red fox darted through a gap in the trees, too fast for him to get more than a glimpse. A fire salamander hid in the leaves at the base of a mossy old beech.

Heinrich found a body of water he'd never seen before, a pond (or perhaps it was a small lake, the requirements for such a designation were not clear to him). There, he caught sight of a grebe of an unfamiliar variety. He brought the pad and pencil from his rucksack and began to sketch it for later research.

It was while he was there sitting in the grass above the water, warm in the midday sun, chewing Braunschweiger and cheese purloined from Oma's kitchen as he scratched busily with his pencil-lead, that he was struck by the feeling of being watched.

He turned his head up, and there, across the water, in the shade of trees, he saw a pale face, long and thin. It looked young, and about the same height off the ground as his, and so Heinrich surmised it belonged to a child.

He raised a hand at the face, deep in the shadows on the other side of the water, and a white hand lifted back at him, as if a reflection. Heinrich closed his notepad, put it back in his rucksack, and started around the water's edge toward the other side.

At the turn on one end of the pond (or small lake), he looked back, but could no longer see the face where it had been. Heinrich stopped, cupped his palms to assist the shade provided by his Tyrolean hat, and trained his vision along the shore.

Then he saw motion in the tops of the trees, the white face and hands moving in the dark, and down a trunk with speed that seemed close to falling until it stopped and the face turned up at him. He saw a white hand wave him closer.

When he stepped into the gloom on the far side of the water, this new forest far darker than his own, Heinrich felt the temperature drop. Much cooler here, out of the sun. He hadn't thought to bring his loden jacket, it having been a warm day on the other side of the water.

He looked about, turning in place, eyes scanning the treetops, but he could not find whatever had been summoning him, or even hear rustling.

Then, as his revolution completed, there was the white face before him, nose nearly touching his own, so close that he surely should have heard the approach, or even smelled it.

"Oh, hello," he said, surprised.

"Hello."

The face belonged, as he'd initially thought, to an especially pale youth, a boy with pronounced and pointed ears, dressed entirely in black. His clothing was of an older style he'd seen in books from a previous era, although the boy looked a bit younger than Heinrich himself.

He was rather smaller than Heinrich had guessed, as well. The height of the face off the ground had been due to a delicate pair of bat-wings on each shoulder, the flapping of which kept him aloft.

Heinrich introduced himself by name, and added that he was a scientist engaged in an expedition.

The boy said that his name was Vladimir, and he was a vampire, and he'd be most excited to join him in his adventure, if he would not be a burden. Heinrich, having been raised to be a polite young scientist, welcomed his new friend, and Vladimir smiled, his teeth a tangle of sharp yellow.

As they tramped through this new, darker forest -- it was Heinrich's boots that made this noise, as Vladimir mostly fluttered -- Heinrich felt he owed it to his new companion to warn him of the potential for danger ahead. He related the stories, how the woman was said to be a witch, and that she was known to abduct children, and possibly cast spells of an unfathomable nature.

He also assured Vladimir that, as a twelve year old man of science, he did not credit such things, and that he would be safe as long as he stayed near Heinrich, whose Opa had taught him how to navigate a forest.

Vladimir thanked him.

However, Heinrich, not quite having known where he was going to begin with, and now in an unfamiliar area, did not know how to proceed. He extracted his compass from his rucksack, but found it to be somehow incapacitated. The arrow just pointed away from Vladimir, no matter which way it was directed. And there was no point bringing out the sextant, as he could not see the horizon, or even the sky in these dense woods.

"Not to worry," Vladimir said. "I think I know where this house is. You said it is constructed of bone and smells of candy and death, yes?"

Heinrich did not recall describing the cottage at all, but agreed that it did sound like something that might have come from the stories. He let Vladimir lead the way.

Giddy at the prospect of being helpful, the younger Vladimir flitted ahead on leathery wings, only to return every few moments to be sure Heinrich was keeping up. Heinrich assured him that he could never be lost in a forest, his or any other, not with the woodsman experience imparted from his Opa, but he appreciated the concern.

They arrived at a clearing in the woods and looked into it. Despite the lack of trees, the sunlight somehow did not filter down into the area.

Heinrich smelled it before he saw the cottage, and it was much as Vladimir had described. Had he not been such a man of science, he might've shivered in superstitious fear.

"Do you think the witch lives there?" Vladimir asked, voice trembling as he hovered behind Heinrich's ear.

"There are no witches," Heinrich responded, and he believed it. "But someone must live there." He could see a pale thread of smoke rising from the bony chimney.

He strode out in to the clearing. Vladimir held back, watching from behind a tree.

Heinrich rapped politely at the door to the cottage. There was a knocker made from what looked like a child-sized human skull, but he elected to use his own knuckles on the wood.

The door creaked slowly open, and a lined face looked out at him, more petrified potato than human. There was a shape behind it, a hump that rose above and a plump and black mass below. A gnarled hand held the handle of the door as a gleaming red eye burned out at him through the shadows. "Yes?"

Heinrich looked at the hand on the door. It was thin and knobby, but he would not have described it as a chicken foot.

He bowed politely and introduced himself. "I am a twelve year old man of science," he explained, "and have come to you to confirm that you are not in fact a witch."

There came a cackle through the doorway that pushed Vladimir deeper into the trees, and might've caused a less scientific mind than Heinrich's to quail in fear. As the hideous laughter became words, he heard:

"The term 'witch' is problematic, with its implication of wickedness, and infers the image of an old crone, which is a hurtful stereotype. Women called witches have always been powerful healers, a status that threatens the heteronormative Christian majority and has in years past led to persecution and violence. Only recently have women of spirituality begun to embrace the term without fear of retribution." The red eye burned out at him, expectant.

"So, then," Heinrich began after a moment, faint confusion marring the confidence customary to his face, "may I infer that you yourself profess no magic powers?"

The old woman's eye glared sharper. "What did I just tell you? There are no magic witches!"

Heinrich smiled to himself. He had known he was right, but it's always nice to have it confirmed.

"Now, 'cannibal' is a word I embrace," the voice went on, "because I do enjoy the flesh of young boys," and the not-chicken-foot hand of the not-witch woman moved out at him, clutching a long knife of sharpened black stone.

"Ah, yes," Heinrich replied, "I suspected as much," and he removed the old but well-maintained revolver from his rucksack and shot the wretched woman through the eye.

It bothered Heinrich that he could not find his own way back, as the forest had grown ever darker and thicker. Vladimir again guided him, this time sticking closer, sometimes flying backwards, his pale face and pointed ears showing almost like a beacon amid the inky trees.

When they reached the body of water, Heinrich invited the vampire boy to come home with him. "Oma's making her strudel," he promised, and oh, how Heinrich did love his Oma's strudel.

"Thank you, but I do not eat," Vladimir said, "strudel."

Heinrich nodded his understanding, although he did not at all understand not eating strudel, and shook Vladimir's cold hand. "You have been an intrepid companion and we must go adventuring again soon."

Vladimir smiled his jagged yellow smile and said, yes, he would like that very much.

It was nearly dark when Heinrich got home, and Oma scolded him for being tardy, but Opa was impressed with the questions his grandson asked about identity politics and the perils of toxic masculinity, and their discussion was lively and enlightening.

Despite her annoyance, Oma served Heinrich three helpings of sauerbraten, and even an extra plate of strudel. He thanked her with a gift of a black, sharpened-stone paring knife he'd brought back from the day's adventure.

He recommended she wash it before use.

HOTEL CARTHAGO

Kim J Cowie

Helen Dodds had not wanted to come on holiday with her parents, but the three of them stood now at the glitzy bar of an upmarket Portuguese hotel. Helen would have preferred to take a holiday with some of her friends, without supervising adults. Portugal appeared ripe with potential for new experiences, but it was disturbingly foreign and she hesitated to shake off the parental leash.

A young woman walked past and glanced at her father. Her mother, Annabel, tugged at her father's jacket. "Who was that woman? She seemed to know you, Henry?" Helen knew that note of disapproval well.

"She's a customer at the bank, that's all," her father snapped. "I don't know what she's doing here."

The stranger was dressed in a dark trouser suit, and had a dangling silver earring at each ear. To Helen's eyes, she appeared to be in her mid to late twenties.

Her mother sniffed; for Helen, the sound carried in it resentment of her dull social life, her husband's stalled career and her fat daughter.

Helen saw an image of herself in a mirror wall: a noticeably bulky girl in an unflattering print dress that suited her neither in cut nor in its colours.

The bar was crowded; a coach had brought another influx of hotel guests, mostly older than Helen's parents and smartly dressed in blazers or summer frocks. Their tanned and lined skin made her think of a colony of lizards.

Her father asked what she wanted to drink. She usually drank diet Coke, but that was boring. "I want a Wild Turkey," said Helen.

"Oh for goodness' sake, Helen! Have a Coca-Cola."

Helen flushed, and could feel sweat between her heavy breasts; she'd have the diet Coke.

Annabel ordered a double gin.

Her father was staring at the tall stranger again, with a look of dislike and apprehension.

The woman was tall and slim; Helen was neither, and her print dress that had seemed adequate for the journey now appeared to her in these elegant surroundings ill-cut and garish.

Her mother had a look on her horsey face again, an expression of discontent with which her daughter was wearily familiar. "I thought you said this hotel was exclusive, Henry."

The next morning, Helen took a walk into the town on her own; for she had found nobody of her own age in the hotel. Her parents wanted to rest by the hotel's pool, but Helen was restless to explore. Perhaps she could discover some new experience here, something improper, of which her mother or father would not approve.

She wore a white cotton skirt and blouse, a straw hat, and high-heeled shoes. When she stood in the main street looking at the map, a local boy soon attached himself to her; he was thin, with black tightly curled hair that shone like wax, the wispy beginnings of a moustache, and a raffish handsomeness. Flattered, she acquiesced.

He introduced himself as Emilio, and showed her the old fort, a relic of the French-British wars, chattering amusingly if, as she suspected, not very accurately about the history of the place.

Later they stood in the Plaza Mayor, a very un-English expanse of dusty paving surrounded on all four sides by weathered buildings of creamy stone, and a great edifice of ornate brickwork. Her guide identified this as the municipal offices. "My uncle, he works there," he informed her proudly. Helen was unimpressed.

Next they visited the basilica, or Se, a cool echoing building filled with oil paintings of saints, and candles. Emilio tried to get her to buy a candle. She refused. They visited the Roman shrine on the hillside above the town. Helen found a leaflet and read it conscientiously. The shrine, with its ugly carvings, was a chilling place. It made her imagine how much blood had been shed here by Romans, Moors and Crusaders. She was finding Emilio's chatter rather irritating. Blood. Now that was interesting.

Hunger gnawed at her, and she thought to return to the hotel and eat, but felt she owed her guide something for his trouble. She thought an offer of money might insult him. Her father had offended the customs men at the airport, and the taxi driver. Foreigners were so touchy.

Helen bought him a drink at a cafe, and they sat at an iron table outside while Emilio bragged about himself. The cafe was crowded; many of the drinkers were of the town; wrinkled faces, wrinkled clothes, weather-tanned skins smelling of sweat and earth. They were short, gnarled men, many no taller than Helen.

Emilio offered to walk her back to her hotel; she found that his route led along a shady alley.

"I live near here," he informed her. "My family will be out. You like to come to my house?"

Helen knew enough to realise why a local youth would chat up a fat English girl rather than one of the Portuguese beauties. With mounting unease, she declined the invitation. Rebuffed, he clamped a hand firmly on her left breast and tried to French kiss her.

Helen struggled, trying to pry him loose. "Stop that!" This was not the sort of holiday romance she had been expecting.

The street was quiet, and not a place frequented by tourists. The buildings of stone and plaster were shuttered, and an old car lay rusting in the shadows. Helen gulped for breath and, heart pounding, looked around for anyone who might help. There was nobody else in sight.

Footsteps sounded behind them. With a flood of relief, Helen recognised the tall dark woman from the hotel, whose name she had pried out of her father. Ms Sheldon raised an elegant eyebrow.

"He's annoying me!" Helen gasped.

Ms Sheldon stepped forward and said something in Portuguese.

With a venomous look, Emilio released Helen and stood with fists clenched, glowering at Sheldon. "Lesbico!" he said, and spat.

Ms Sheldon's half-clenched hand struck the youth across the face with a bone-crunching smack. He staggered. Blood trickled from a cut lip.

He swore, and pulled out a knife from inside his jacket. He turned it slowly, and the handsome Iberian features became ugly and vicious. Helen squealed, but Sheldon merely watched him. Suddenly she leapt forward and struck the knife away with her left arm while kicking him between the legs, again very hard. He doubled up with a gasp of pain and shock.

By the time he straightened, she had picked up the knife. "Stupid," said Ms Sheldon. She moved towards the youth slowly, tossing the knife into her other hand and holding it ready for a stab. When she was almost in reach, he looked into her eyes, whirled with a cry of fear and fled down the alley, with a slight hobbling gait.

"Oh thanks!" cried Helen. "That was amazing!" She had not liked the groping, but Ms Sheldon's violence excited her in a way she found hard to express.

Sheldon folded the knife and slipped it out of sight. She took Helen's hand. "You should be more careful. I'll take you back to your hotel."

"It was awful. He was so nice before."

"What's your name?"

Helen told her.

Ms Sheldon glanced at Helen's high-heeled open shoes. "You should wear trainers, Helen, then if it happens again you can try running away."

"Were you really going to knife him up?"

"Better not to ask. I don't like little boys who talk back to me. And don't mention knives to anyone else, you hear?"

"I think you're amazing. My dad couldn't do anything like that."

Helen encountered her parents in the hotel's red and gilt wallpapered downstairs hallway.

"Why did you come back here with that woman, Helen?" her father demanded.

"A boy was annoying me and she chased him off. She was terrific."

"You've two buttons missing, Helen," her mother cried. Helen hadn't noticed. "What did he do?"

She rolled her eyes. "He was pawing me and tried to stick his tongue in my mouth. It was dire."

"How did you get mixed up with this boy?" her father asked.

"He offered to show me around the town. He seemed perfectly nice at first, till he invited me to his house and I refused."

"I think we ought to inform the police," said her father.

"Jessica says that wouldn't be a good idea at all. You'd spend half the holiday at the Policia barracks filling in forms while they made dirty remarks about my virtue."

"Does she?" her father scowled.

"She's got her own jewellery business that's doing really well and she's very clever and got really good taste in clothes," Helen rattled on.

"You seem to be taking this attack very calmly," said Annabel. She rearranged Helen's blouse neck.

"It's no worse than things that happen at school," said Helen, as they entered the dining room.

Her mother frowned.

"You'd better not leave the hotel on your own again," said her father.

"Are you going to come with me instead? I thought you didn't want to trek around in the blazing sun?"

They took a table and her father signalled to a waiter.

Her father sighed. "We can go when it's cooler."

"Why can't I go with Ms Sheldon?"

Her father choked.

"She can't be that bad if she's a customer at your bank. She's clearly got lots of money. She doesn't remember you, Daddy," Helen added.

In the end however, her parents agreed Helen could associate with Ms Sheldon.

That afternoon Helen watched as Jessica Sheldon, lean and fit and elegant in stretch Lycra, performed rowing exercises on the machines in the hotel's health suite. The suite, with white concrete walls and sprung floors, was in the basement. Jessica had a small gold earring dangling from each ear.

"Why don't you go and put on a pair of pants and a T-shirt, Helen?" Jessica said. "We'll try getting you fit."

Soon, she pinched Helen's thigh as the girl sat on a cycle trainer. "You're a fat little thing." She beckoned to the health assistant. "Giorgio? See that she doesn't strain herself."

Helen, who had always been plump, normally assiduously avoided exercise. From the cycle machine, Giorgio transferred her to a rowing machine where she puffed and struggled. "It all hurts," she complained.

Next morning, before the sun got too high, Jessica Sheldon set out on a run along the damp sands of the beach. Helen, whose hair was now tied back in an imitation of Jessica's, trotted after her. After a few hundred yards, Helen made a cry of despair.

"I can't go on, I'm dying!" She clutched her side.

"Don't stop, keep walking," Jessica said kindly. "I'll collect you on my way back." And she set off at a steady lope.

Jessica returned ten minutes later and collected Helen, who trailed after her doggedly before collapsing on the esplanade steps.

Jessica ruffled Helen's hair. "You'll feel better when you've run more often," she said. "What do you eat, Helen?"

"Everything," said Helen with a sigh.

"You know what's fattening. Stop eating it."

Helen returned for breakfast at nine-thirty. She wolfed the coffee and rolls, but stopped herself from reaching for the croissants.

"What have you been doing this morning?" her father asked.

"I went for a run on the beach. With Jessica."

Dodds failed to conceal his surprise.

"Helen, I am still not sure that Ms Sheldon is a suitable companion for a young girl."

"Why's that? She's not old, she's from England and she knows the town."

"I just think she's not a suitable person," Dodds floundered.

"You met her before. Do you mean she might be a lesbian, Daddy?" Helen said, enjoying the shock value of this reply. "You should approve of her; she's got loads of money."

"I'm sorry if you're not having a very good time, Helen. I know you wanted a holiday without us, but your mother and I -"

"I'm a big girl, Daddy. Stop fussing."

That evening, Dodds and his wife discussed their daughter.

"Are you sure that woman's a suitable acquaintance?" Annabel Dodds asked. "Look what's happened to Helen's hair. It's been ruined, all tied back in a messy bundle. And she looks dreadful in those shorts, that show her podgy legs. You should speak to her."

"Helen won't listen; she's got a crush on that woman," Dodds complained. He shuddered at the memory of the brush with his daughter earlier in the day.

"I do hope not." Annabel Dodds said with a scowl. "But it's an improvement on street boys." A half-bottle of gin stood opened on the white and gold bedside table. It had been three-quarters drained, and beside it stood a glass with red lipstick marks on its rim.

Jessica took Helen on an expedition into the old fishing village, where they looked at and tried on jewellery, and entered a dim cafe where they drank strong frothy coffee and Jessica carried on whispered conversations with strangers. The same strangers asked Helen if she had a boyfriend and if she liked Jessica very much.

"Boys are only interested in one thing. I like Jessica a lot."

They found her replies very amusing.

Someone got up and put a few escudos in the juke-box in the corner, an old Wurlitzer.

"What's that gloomy music?" Helen said.

"Amalia Rodrigues, I think," said Jessica.

It appeared to Helen that most of Jessica's acquaintances wore Italian suits and sunglasses. Sometimes they talked of money, and sometimes they spoke Portuguese so she couldn't understand a word they said.

After a lunch of caldo verde soup and pork, they visited the house of one of Jessica's friends, secluded behind wrought-iron railings. Their host, a pale-suited man, collected curios and claimed to be a magician, an expert in Carthaginian and Phoenician magic. Helen was intrigued.

His rooms were tall and dingy, with tapestries and old paintings on the walls, and cabinets filled with stone tools, shrunken heads, grotesque idols and the like. The conversation took a curious turn. They were talking of prehistoric stone ruins, and earth magic, and someone mentioned magic that had come over from Africa with the Carthaginians.

Helen giggled. Their pale-suited host rose, moved to a corner of the room, and opened a cabinet made of dark wood. He took Helen's left hand, and passed a bracelet of metal over her wrist, and adjusted its position. It pressed at a point on her wrist, and stimulated her body, as though blood was flowing faster. The sensation reminded her, disagreeably, of a party at which a boy had given her something to smoke.

Into her right hand the man placed a smooth and curiously shaped stone, of an olive green colour. It fitted into the palm of her hand, and her fingers rubbed it. The adults continued their conversation in a desultory way, but she knew they were watching her. Helen became aware of the sensations of sex. She could not stop rubbing the stone, sensed herself blushing, could not stop rubbing the stone. Their voices came as if from a great distance. She was intensely conscious of the warmth in her sexual organs.

"What do you want, Helen?" asked the pale-suited man.

"I- " Words stuck in her throat. She wanted many things, among them, not to be humiliated by boys.

"She wants power," said Jessica's voice.

"She shall have it."

Helen could not stop caressing the stone. The room blurred before her eyes as she trembled to the energy in her body. A dam of pleasure burst. She stopped rubbing.

She awoke suddenly with a headache. She had been asleep in an old padded chair that smelt musty. Her recollections were confused, of stones, of necklaces of bone.

One of Jessica's mysterious friends was near her. The woman straightened quickly, and walked out to a sunlit patio. Helen examined her own plump hand. It stung, and she was almost sure there was a puncture mark there.

She rubbed at it angrily, a little frightened. Dared she complain? Speak to Jessica? What if it had been only an insect - then she'd look stupid and all these clever, elegant people would only laugh at her. She was relieved when Jessica came for her almost at once and proposed that they go out to visit the Convent museum.

It was now three in the afternoon. They walked down streets of muted commerce, that smelled of exhaust fumes, before passing through a wooden door in a larger gate into the arched cloisters of the seventeenth century convent.

"What happened when he put that bracelet on my arm?" Helen asked with unease.

Jessica stopped and met her eyes. "You should not have laughed when Lurio spoke of the old Carthaginian magic. Perhaps he has done something to you, perhaps not."

Involuntarily Helen dropped a hand to the crotch of her shorts. Jessica saw it. "No, nothing like that. You will know, sooner or later, if he has."

"It was beastly," said Helen, and instantly regretted it, for she sensed Jessica had been about to say more. Helen found herself half hoping that something strange and exciting had been done to her. Jessica turned, reached back for Helen's hand and drew her onwards over worn flagstones.

That afternoon they spent an hour in the quiet, dusty halls of the Convent museum, looking at canvasses darkened by age. Jessica took her through tall oaken doors into a dusty room where hung artworks in worm-eaten gilt frames, all showing some kind of abnormality. Freaks, dwarves, microcephalitic idiots, manticores, demons.

"Lurio told me about this place," Jessica said.

Helen stopped before the last painting. "This one looks quite normal. I don't understand."

"Vagina Dentata," Jessica said. "It's a legend, of women who had two sets of teeth; one in the usual place and the others, somewhere else."

In the cool of the end of the day, they sat in a quiet cobbled square before walking back through streets of old stone houses to the hotel for dinner. Helen sensed something burning inside her.

In the evening they attended a disco in another hotel. Jessica danced to local rock music by Rui Velaso; brilliantly, Helen thought. Helen soon excused herself and returned to her hotel. She slept heavily.

Helen sat on the concrete wall that bounded the lush garden in front of the hotel. She wore a blood-red miniskirt, the warm blockwork rough under her legs. She waited. Taxis drew into the Paradisio driveway and left. Local people, wrinkled by sun, ambled lazily by. A few tourists in bright clothes hurried in or out of the hotel.

After half an hour, a youth appeared. His features were Portuguese, handsome, sullen, his hair African. He walked slowly towards the hotel. When he sighted Helen he paused, then seeing that she was alone came on at the same pace as before. His face assumed a half-smile, mocking and superior. Helen sat still, her face expressionless. The boy stopped before her. "Ah, Signora!"

He glanced up and down the empty, dusty road. He smiled, without warmth, and stepped close to her. His hands closed on her shoulders. Her eyes met his. He faltered a little at the expression of deep contempt in them, then thrust his face forward and pressed his lips hard on hers. She did not resist, did not move.

"Good, Signora," the boy murmured. He moved a hand to squeeze her breast through the thin blouse and her brassiere. Helen touched his slim body through the shirt. It was warm, and vibrating. When he came up for air, she lowered her head and looked down; his manhood had risen and was swelling out the front of the tight trousers.

Her lips brushed his neck. "Signora!"

She found flesh, and bit hard, breaking the skin with her sharp teeth.

He yelled and tried to pull away, to strike her, but with her new strength she held him for a second. It was enough. The body became rigid, vibrating, and his face distorted into pain and terror. He was screaming faintly, thinly.

She put a foot up on the wall and heaved the youth up after her, gripping him under the armpits. She peered up and down the street. It was still empty. She pulled the body among the tall bushes of the hotel garden and propped it against the lower branches of an olive tree. The boy was paralysed, but still alive. She bent to undo the fly of the trousers and pull down the white underpants. The penis sprang out, tumescent, glans exposed, and with a translucent bead of mucus gleaming at the tip.

A scream tore faintly up the bitten neck. "No! No! No!" The body quivered with terror as the trapped boy strove vainly to escape.

Helen stifled the screams with her strong hands. She raised her skirt and squatted over the hard penis. The olive branches began to bounce. A shrill squeak of agony and despair escaped from between her throttling hands. Blood soaked the crotch of the opened trousers and dribbled to the ground.

When she had finished, she dragged the now limp body further into the shrubbery where it could not be seen, and wiped blood from her thighs with a tissue. She threw the tissue to the ground, slipped over the wall to the quiet road and re-entered the hotel. Nobody gave her more than a glance as she walked across the lobby to the lifts and pressed the call button. The slide doors slithered back, and she stepped into an empty lift. In the upper corridor there was only a dark-haired maid, servicing rooms at the far end. Her parents were out, looking at the town Museum.

She undressed and showered herself carefully, washing away all the blood. She rubbed herself, sighing with remembered pleasure.

The following evening Helen, now clad in green cycling shorts and a leather jacket, went with Jessica to a fado house.

"What's that?" Helen had asked when Jessica had suggested this outing.

Jessica had explained with a certain asperity. "I don't know why your parents bothered bringing you here. Bognor would have done as well." They sat in a corner of a dim cafe while a lot of passionate Portuguese singing filled Helen's ears. Wine bottles stood on most of the tables, and Jessica held a whispered conversation with someone in dark glasses.

A glass of strong dark wine made Helen talkative. Iberian faces hissed at her to be quiet. She thought it was all rather dull, though Jessica evidently enjoyed the wild, gloomy music a lot.

"Have you seen any more of Emilio?" Jessica asked in a low voice.

"No. Another boy showed up outside the hotel, and I had him."

"Your first love-bite? What was it like?" Jessica asked as if they were discussing ice-cream.

Helen had not intended to tell even Jessica what she had done; but she was unable to resist the questioning and gave way to her own compulsion to tell. Her words poured out as she described everything; what she had done, and how she had felt. "It was good. He went stiff, as though he was plugged into electricity. And his screaming made me want to come."

She chattered on till the waiter sidled towards them with their order, and Jessica placed a warning finger over Helen's lips. "Hush! No one must ever suspect what you are. It will be deadly for you."

Helen, delivered back to the hotel at midnight, slept soundly till the early hours when she was disturbed by nightmare. She dreamed that a dark thing from Roman times was pursuing her.

At seven she rose, with a throbbing hangover, showered, and joined Jessica Sheldon for a run along the deserted beach, along the sands exposed by the tide. Neither of them, by unspoken consent, referred to the previous events.

At breakfast, Helen's parents asked her what she had done the previous night. "Listened to fado," was the terse reply.

After breakfast, Helen felt much better. She walked alone into the town, dressed now in a light dress with a brocade waistcoat over it, heavily embroidered. She still wore the training shoes. She took a guidebook with her and looked again at the basilica and the Roman ruins. None of the local boys looked at her. A new strength buoyed her mood.

In the basilica she found no presence of God, only the old things that had come over from the Dark Continent, stirring under her feet, whispering to her, calling to her infected blood.

Next day a body had been found in the hotel grounds and police and reporters swarmed around like flies. Jessica watched from behind a screen of sunflowers as the Dodds' luggage was piled, days ahead of schedule, into a taxi, and fat Helen, dressed in a sleeveless vest and tight Lycra shorts, and her short hair brushed up into a quiff stiff with grease, was being dragged into it by her father. Helen's face was set in a mutinous pout.

Jessica Sheldon smiled.

THE BIG EMPTY

Wayne Kyle Spitzer

Photographers call it the golden hour, that period of time right before sunset when the sky glows orange and the shadows lose their edges, and the world becomes, for the space of about 20 minutes, something elevated and painterly—ephemeral, even sublime. Add to that the ocean breaking over the rocks and the black and white 19th century lighthouse, and, well, you have some idea of how seeing Granite Point that first time affected us (when we were taking it all in by Jeep, whose top we'd removed in spite of the pterodactyls swarming the beach). So, too, were there the strange lights in the sky, which peered down, relentlessly, disapprovingly, as though we had no right to even celebrate (by going on what Amelia had called our "post-apocalyptic honeymoon"), nor to end our crushing isolation.

Beyond that, though, beyond the fact that it was the golden hour and the waves were crashing and that one side of the lighthouse gleamed like polished brass (or that we were still euphoric over having encountered each other less than 24 hours before), beyond all that was our shared epiphany; which was that the lantern, far from being illuminated from without, was, now that we'd had a chance to observe it up close, shining from within. That it had somehow been kept on—either by electricity or gas or the burning of oil or kerosene—and that it would have had to have been carefully maintained. Which meant that someone, somehow, someone just like us, perhaps, had managed to survive.

"It's beautiful," said Amelia—and swallowed, batting away the tears. "My God, Francis. Look at it. I never thought—"

"That you'd see a light again, I know." I peered at the house attached to the tower's base and the old truck parked in its drive—which looked to be in surprisingly good shape. "Nor did I." I looked at her sidelong and gave her a little wink. "But then, I didn't expect *you,* either."

She didn't notice, only continued staring at the lantern house, as if she were in a daze. "It shifts ... the light. First white, then blue, then purple. And then a color—sort of like bottle green, only iridescent. Like a mallard's neck. And yet shot through with ..."

She looked at me as if for help.

"Beats me," I said. "I'm color blind. Red-green color deficiency. Either way, I suggest we make contact—if we're going to. It'll be too dangerous after dark."

She seemed to come out of it, whatever *it* was. "Is that a good idea? I mean, with just our knives?"

"No," I said, studying the darkened house. "But—whoever they are—they're using *something* for power." I lifted my gaze to the rotating lamp. "Enough to turn and illuminate that thing. And I'd like to know what it is." I looked at her across the cab, which was bathed in golden light. "Wouldn't you?"

And we just stared at each other: there by the lighthouse at Granite Point on the Oregon coast, after the time-storm—the Flashback, as someone had called it at the beginning—the dinosaur apocalypse. After everyone had vanished and the entire world had become a landscape of cycads and ruins, a place inhabited by winds and the souls of winds, a lost country.

"Jesus. Just—Jesus," said Amelia, staring at the decomposing body. "How long do you think it's been here?"

I examined it where it was sprawled on the back porch, facing the ocean, its skin blackened and clinging to the bones—like it had been vacuum sealed—its wispy hair fluttering. "Hard to say. Few weeks. Maybe a month." I batted away the flies. "Long enough for the organs to liquify."

"How—how do you know?"

I studied the holes in its head, a smaller one which was about the size of a dime and a larger, more cavernous one—the exit wound. "Because, otherwise, there'd be brains all over." I stepped over it and picked up the gun, checked its chamber. "There's still bullets in it."

She stared at me tentatively as I closed the chamber and gripped the weapon in both hands—neither of us saying anything. At last I nodded to the back door—the screen of which banged back and forth in the wind—and tried to brace myself. "You ready?"

She shook her head.

"Let's go," I said.

And then she was holding the screen as I inched forward and gripped the knob—turning it slowly, carefully, easing the door open. Stepping into a room which was dark as pitch; which reeked of cat piss and despair.

We worked well together, that much was clear; it was evidenced by how we swept and cleared the house so efficiently, Amelia opening the curtains (to let in more light) even as I scrambled to quick-check the rooms and closet spaces—finding a radio with batteries in it as well as some flashlights; not to mention a pantry full of food (mainly jars and jars of canned fish—salmon and snapper, according to the labels). Still, what I *didn't* find was any evidence of a non-electric power source for the lantern; something which seemed impossible—given the grid had failed shortly after the Flashback and the house itself was completely inert. Nor would this have gone unexamined—that is, if not for the discovery of the door; by which I mean the padlocked door to the tower itself, which we stumbled across at virtually the same instant—or so it seemed—having found it tucked away in a kind of antechamber in the furthermost section of the home.

"But, why the hell would he lock it?" I confess I was flummoxed.

Amelia frowned. "Why wouldn't he? He probably felt as though he were the only one that—I don't know, could be trusted with it. To maintain it. Especially after the Flashback." She fingered a small hook next to the door. "That's odd—don't you think?"

I stared at the hook. It was the only thing that *wasn't.*

"It's probably on that corpse; the key, I mean."

She looked up at me fetchingly, her brown eyes—she said they were green—flicking up and down my body, once, twice.

"Now wait just a damn minute,"

"Now you wouldn't promise me a lighthouse and then fail to deliver, would you?" She ran her hands over my shirt and up the sides of my neck, cupping my face in her palms, tilting her head. "I mean, we *are* on our honeymoon—aren't we? And who knows what a girl might do if escorted to the top of that beautiful beacon with the waves crashing all around her and the seabirds–"

"Pterodactyls," I corrected her. "They're pterodactyls. And they'll peck your eyes out."

"Whatever," she rasped, and brushed my lips with her own. "What are you afraid of? That you'll catch the Ebola virus? Or maybe smallpox? The 1918 flu?"

"What I'm afraid of," I lowered her hands gently. "Is that we're going to lose the light and get stuck here. Like, all night." I looked at her sternly. "And I don't think you want that."

She picked at and adjusted my shirt collar, undeterred. "Why not? I mean, where else should we go? Back to Walmart? Back to those little settees in Home Furnishings, with their hard, hard little cushions—where you were such a gentleman, I might add, to just talk to me and assuage my doubts, and to not try so much as a—"

There was a sound, a kind of warbling yowl, a drawn-out, caterwauling, doleful cry, which rose up from the nearby trees and reverberated along the shoreline—where it was promptly answered by another, and yet another.

Neither of us moved.

At last I said: "That was a pit raptor."

Nobody said anything as the waves crashed against the rocks and the pterodactyls squawked.

"Out on the point? That's impossible."

"No, it's not. They're night hunters. They're just beginning their workday."

"But—"

"Shhh. Listen."

The sound came again—briefer, this time, more succinct, as though the animal was moving.

I looked around the room—my heart pounding, but there were no windows, no way to tell what was going on outside. "We've got to go. Like, now. Before—"

"But, don't you see? That's what I was trying to tell you. *We took the top down."*

I froze, feeling as though the walls were closing in—like I might actually pass out. But then—then it just passed, I can't really explain it, and I was myself again (the "cool cucumber," as Amelia had described me), and what's more, I'd accepted it. Accepted that I had led us blunderingly into a bad situation because I had hoped, in some dim quarter of my mind—and this despite it being the end of the world itself—to make time with her.

Amelia. The girl I'd met in a ruined Walmart in Coos Bay while scrounging for a pair of shoes—again, while the sun was going down—as well as something to eat. I guess one didn't know whether to laugh or to cry. Either way, one thing had become clear. And that was that, for this night, anyway—we weren't going anywhere.

Now, you might ask: Didn't I find it odd that she'd be so adamant on sleeping separately—in spite of the cold and her earlier flirtatiousness—that we had to drag a bed into the antechamber? And my answer is: No. Not really. Rather, I just took it to mean she was establishing a boundary, and that the apocalypse itself couldn't turn her into something she wasn't—which, frankly, I respected. Besides, any man who knows anything knows the coin paid going in is the same earned staying out, which is to say Time, however scrambled it had become, was on my side, and I knew it.

More than any of that, though, was that I wanted to try out the radio, which I did, drinking scotch from the caretaker's stash and looking out the window—which framed the breakers and gathered pterodactyls like a picture—wrapped in one of the keeper's thick, filthy blankets. At which I was delighted to discover that the batteries were good and that it in fact worked—and so began scrubbing the dial; hoping, against hope, to catch something, anything (an emergency broadcast signal, a test tone, *anything*) but finding only static; until, suddenly, even as I was about to give up, there were a flurry of sounds—sounds such as I hadn't heard since before the Flashback—which, taken together, constituted a thing I'd thought no longer possible, a thing as extinct as the terrible lizards themselves, which I turned down immediately in order to keep all to myself, and soaked up as though fresh from the desert—marinating in it, breathing it all in, drowning.

Woah, Georgia ... Geoorrgia ... No peace, no peace I find. Just an old, sweet song, keeps Georgia, on my miiind ....

I think I must have sunk to the floor, sunk to it in a veritable puddle, spilling the bottle of scotch which clinked and sloshed, forgetting about the cold and the lantern and the pit raptors—which may or may not have still been out there—forgetting the lost country and its hopelessness.

I said just an old, sweet song, keeps Georgia ... on my miiind ...

Until it was over, and the instruments and back-up singers had all faded to nothing, and a voice came on—a new voice, a speaking voice; a *woman's* voice—and said, mellifluously, "And that was the immortal Ray Charles, with "Georgia on my Mind." And this—this is Radio Free Montana—with Bella Ray, broadcasting from Barley Hot Springs in what some used to call the Great White North—which was not intended as a compliment." She laughed. "So just trust in God and keep your powder dry; and stay with us here wherever you may be—whether that's a cold water flat in Devil's Lake, North Dakota, or a high-rise hotel in Miami-Dade—wherever you are out there in the Big Empty, we here at KAAR-RFM will try to have your back. And now it's back to the music and Patsy Cline, with "Walking After Midnight." Take it away, Patsy!"

I was up and moving down the hall almost before I'd realized it, double-timing it for Amelia's room, using one of the flashlights I'd found to see the way, knocking on her door (which seemed thick as a vault now that I thought about it and just sort of absorbed the sound, like solid rock).

Jesus, I remember thinking. I'd searched for a mere signal and found a whole community! It was like we'd gotten rescued from *Gilligan's Island;* escaped from the *Land of the Lost.* Like we'd come home from Oz itself. And I simply couldn't wait to tell her— although how the music hadn't awakened her was completely beyond me. I mean, surely—

But she didn't answer the door, which seemed impossible, not even when I pounded on it with my fists, which literally shook off paint peelings. "Amelia!" I shouted. "Amelia!" I pounded again and again. "Wake up, Amelia!"

Until at last I thought, *Fuck this,* and tried the knob—only to find it locked. At which I resolved to kick it in (fat chance), or find an ax (she could be dying in there!), and was backing away from it to try just that, when it occurred to me I was acting like a psychopath and a fool.

The fact was, she was a heavy sleeper, I'd seen it myself the previous night. And she was in the habit of wrapping the pillow about her head, which would have further blunted any sound. And that door—Jesus Christ.

I wandered back into the living room and turned off the radio, to conserve the batteries. It would just have to wait until morning, like digging the key out of the corpse's pocket. The fact was—everything was going to be all right. And with that I found another bottle of liquor—Jeppson's Malört, whatever the fuck that was—and settled in on the couch; after which the grandfather clock struck 8 and what looked a plesiosaur, only huge, like a small whale, leapt from the ocean—to snatch one of the pterodactyls from the orange-painted rocks.

"What, you've never wondered if you dreamt something or actually experienced it? Happens to me. And you said it yourself: you were shit-canned off that—what was it?"

"Jeppson's Malört," I said—still tasting it in my mouth, smelling it on my sweat. Still feeling as though it had been poured over my brain like bile. "Look, it wasn't a dream, okay?"

I stopped walking and stared at her—to emphasize my point—as seabirds swirled (there were no pterodactyls today) and the waves crashed. "Look, I know it's hard to believe, but I'm telling you: Someone is on the air." I gripped her shoulders—harder than I'd intended. "Radio Free Montana—that's what they call themselves. Broadcasting out of a place called Barley Hot Springs. Jesus, Amelia. Don't you see what that means?"

She placed her hands on her hips. "Have you listened to yourself?" She briefly put her face in her palm. "How would a signal even get from there to here, without—I don't know, a relay of some kind. What you're saying is *crazy,* Francis—can't you see that?" She shook her head as if in pity. "I mean, can't you?"

"I'm not crazy," I said, and took my hands off her. "I heard what I heard. And we've got to go there—like, now, today. While the sun is shining. I swear, I'll—" I looked back at the lighthouse and the old truck parked near our Jeep. "I'll go alone if I have to."

She picked up a couple pieces of driftwood, first one, then the other, looking exasperated. "Then why aren't they broadcasting anymore? Riddle me that, Francis. And why aren't you gathering wood for the fire? For that matter; why aren't you burying our friend?"

"There's maggots," I said—and started walking, finding it strange she hadn't mentioned the key. "I'm working up to it. And to hell with the fire. You're just trying to change the subject."

"Oh, I see. Well—isn't that what we came out here for? To gather wood?" She hurried to catch up with me. "Or would you prefer to freeze again tonight? You know: and to pickle yourself in Jeppson's Merlot, like—"

"Malört," I said, increasing my pace. "Besides, I don't plan on being here. And neither should you."

She stopped abruptly and called after me, "Then where are you going?"

I took a few more steps and then paused—but didn't turn around. "I was just walking—if you want to know the truth. Figured it would do us some good. But now—now I want to look at *that."* And I pointed.

At the beach grasses which had been singed and lain down nearly flat—as if a burning helicopter had set down directly in their midst—and the saltbushes twisted into an insidious vortex. At the mounds and mounds of sand and other sediment which had been dredged up and redeposited—in an approximate circle—by some presently unseen force (a bulldozer, perhaps); or an object from space having made sudden, violent impact.

"What do you suppose it was?" asked Amelia, poking the ashy dirt with one of her sticks, stirring it around.

"I wouldn't do that," I warned. "Could be unexploded ordinance—you never know."

She gasped and moved back—although not very far—as I studied the point of impact, noting how angular it was, how geometrical (as if a giant arrowhead had been stabbed into the earth); all of which left me to wonder—had the object somehow been removed? Or was it still down there?

I scanned the area, looking for debris. "There's no wreckage—which is odd. So I doubt it was a satellite. No; I'm afraid there's only two possibilities, really. Bomb or meteorite. And I doubt very much it was a bomb."

"Or *is?*"

"Or is."

She didn't say anything, only continued staring into the dirt.

At last I said, "What is it?"

"Nothing ... it ... it's nothing." She seemed dazed, confused. "It's just that ... it all seems so strange now. I mean—that we ever had use for such things. For bombs. That we could spend so much time and effort and money ... just to kill each other."

She looked out at the ocean and the billowing clouds, the whirling seabirds, the distant pterodactyls. "That we could make such ugliness and pain—such sheer terror—and in such a beautiful world. I mean, *look* at it, Francis. Can you honestly say that it's not better off without us? Or that, even if there are other people, we're not better off without them?"

I must have looked confused. "What the hell are you talking about?"

She turned to face me; her dark eyes close to mine. "Give me one reason, Francis. Give me one reason why we shouldn't just stay here, forever—you and I, alone. Give me one reason why we shouldn't restore the lighthouse and defend it and kill anyone who comes close; why we shouldn't go so far as to kill them first—just kill them where they sleep—and stop the threat before it even begins. Tell me now why they're worth saving, and why we shouldn't finish what *they* started," She nodded briskly at the sky, "What they instigated with the Flashback but failed to complete. What can be completed still—"

And I kissed her, suddenly, completely—I'm still not sure why, maybe because I thought she was breaking down and that doing so would be the only way to snap her out of it, to shock her back to her senses. All I know is that she responded almost immediately and we stayed like that for some time, kissing not as children lost in a storm—which is how it had felt that first night when she'd pecked me on the lips before retreating to her own settee—but as something akin to red hot lovers: thirstily, intensely, primally (but not base), the Bogie and Bacall of the apocalypse.

After which I said, "Maybe you shouldn't be alone tonight."

And she said: "Not yet." And then kissed me again.

Until the moment (and the day) had passed and we'd agreed to stay one more night, and she'd retired by 8 pm to the antechamber while I drank vodka on the couch, shortly after which a plesiosaur breached the froth like a glistening killer whale—and snatched a pterodactyl from the orange-painted rocks.

I'm not going to lie; I hadn't really expected to find it—the key—regardless of what I'd expressed previously; so, imagine my surprise when I searched the corpse's stained pockets—managing, somehow, to keep a tenuous grasp on my breakfast—and touched a crenulated edge.

Bingo, I remember thinking, not lastly because it seemed to absolve Amelia—whom I'd come to suspect had taken it and not told me—but also because it would allow me to test something;

something I'd been thinking about a lot since discovering the strange crater. One of *many* things I'd been thinking about.

I peered up at the lantern as the rain fell and the clouds drifted, as the melancholy of the day hung over everything like a shroud. *Tell me now why humanity is worth saving, and why we shouldn't finish what They started. What They instigated with the Flashback but failed to complete. What can be completed still.*

The words sat on my stomach like poached eggs. Absolved her? Perhaps. But not explained anything.

I gazed along the beach: at the desolate breakers and the gray tide rolling in, at the vortex of saltbushes about a half mile away—flies buzzing my face as I did so. I wasn't ready for this shit. For burying the lighthouse keeper. Then I started walking (wondering, as I went, what the weather was like in Montana, and if they had children there—and if so, were they happy and well-provided for?) ... until at last I came to the crater; where I quickly noticed something which should have been obvious the day before (but somehow hadn't been), and that was that it was incredibly close to the road itself—and that, indeed, they were separated only by a sandy embankment. An embankment, I soon realized, which still had drag marks in it—as though someone had unearthed whatever had fallen and pulled it up to the road.

I looked back the way I'd come—the rain pelting my jacket, the wind buffeted my hair.

As though someone had loaded it onto a truck; and then driven it—not bothering to pass "Go" or to collect $200—back to the lighthouse at Granite Point.

"Amelia?" I knocked on her door gently but firmly. "The Jeep's all ready to go. Also, I—I buried the keeper. I mean it's pretty shallow, but ... it'll have to do."

I waited a moment to see if she'd answer. When she didn't, I added: "And there's something else. Something I want to show you."

Still no answer. Only the breathing of the ocean, the ticking of the grandfather clock. I knocked again.

"Amelia? *Hey.* You there?"

That's when I knew. That's when I knew she'd had the key all along—had it since before I'd even discovered the antechamber; since she'd found it on the hook next to the lighthouse door—and that she must have planted it on the keeper only recently, possibly even the previous night.

And then I was turning the knob and the door was opening—just swinging in as easy as could be—and my shadow had fallen across her bed which was piled with blankets and clothes; after which, sweating and trembling, I looked at the lighthouse door—and saw that it was lazed open.

And began to move toward it.

I saw it even before I saw her—a spearpoint-shaped thing, an impossible thing, a thing blacker than black yet giving off light—which levitated straight as an arrow at the center of the Fresnel and somehow caused it to turn, to warp, to change its shape and then back again, to be at once physical yet abstract. Nor was it the size of even the largest lightbulbs but rather tall as a man, with no surface features whatsoever—like one of those cars which has been painted Vantablack and so absorbs all incidental light—a thing as perfect as it was paradoxical, and which had no color of its own yet somehow radiated multitudes.

A thing beyond which—out on the catwalk—stood Amelia: barefoot but wrapped in the keeper's bathrobe; facing away from the black light and myself; facing the sea which rose up and crashed on the rocks.

I circled around toward her but paused, gripping the doorframe. "H-Hello? Amelia? What—what are you doing out there? Are you okay?"

She didn't respond, only continued facing the sea (and the seabirds, which swirled like moths), her hair whipping and lashing—pulsing and glowing—appearing as though it were on fire as I crept onto the catwalk and approached her with caution. As she dropped the robe from her body—revealing herself to be completely nude—and I reached for her shoulder, slowly turning her around.

At which she said, "Careful, it'll eat your eyes," and looked up at me with eyes that had become black glass—like black, interstellar voids—and yet, *not,* because they were also full of light; full of pulsars and quasars and nebulae and supernovae; of blue giants and red dwarfs and white fountains and stellar flares—and colors which could not be defined much less comprehended—hues I should not have been able to see but could!

All of which was the moment I looked at the clouds and understood—and knew at once what the queer object was—for it was nothing less than one of the strange lights in the sky; nothing less than one of the architects of the Flashback itself—one that had fallen to Earth like a shooting star and been recovered by the lighthouse keeper after the Collapse (and which he had then placed inside his Fresnel). One that had gotten into Amelia and was in her even now, whispering to her, I realized—even as I backed into the lantern house and she quickly followed—guiding her. Compelling her toward some end I hadn't the ability to imagine.

"You see it—I can tell you do," she said, having followed my gaze; having focused on the lights in the clouds, on *them*—whose colors were the same as those in her eyes. "You see it and yet do not fully understand it." She looked at me and tilted her head; began touching my lips, tracing them as though they were art. "Let it in, Francis. Let it in as I will let you in—here, now, in every way."

She lowered to her knees—smoothly, silkily—sliding her hands along my body, unfastening my pants. "They have work for us." She pushed up my shirt and began kissing my stomach.

"Do it with me, Francis. Do the work. You said it yourself—they're in Montana. Take me there."

And then she was gripping me and taking me into her mouth, moving her lips up and down, as I put her head in my hands and looked at the thing, the anomaly, the perfect, black arrowhead which somehow emanated light, and which showed me things even as I looked at it—dreadful things, horrible things—images in which people were being murdered by their own trust and generosity; visions in which I saw an entire community lain to waste. Until I could take it no more—for it was the future I saw—and tore myself away: yanking up my trousers and hurrying for the hatch, clambering down the spiral staircase which pulsed and flashed with light, bursting into the antechamber and down the hall into the living room.

Where I snatched up a bottle of whisky and began drinking it raw and undiluted. Where I crumbled to the floor and moaned, wondering what to think or do.

They call it the golden hour, that period of time right before sunset when the sky glows orange and the shadows lose their edges, and the world becomes, for the space of about 20 minutes, something elevated and painterly—ephemeral, even sublime. That's how the world felt as I sat on the rocks and watched the waves crash and spume—*sublime.* A thing of such grandeur and beauty that we couldn't help but to stand in awe. And yet, at the same time, weren't we part and parcel? Weren't we built of the same materials—the same *substantia primae*—and woven into its fabric like threads? And—that being the case—weren't we special too?

"You know it's funny," said Amelia, her voice sounding distant, muted, as though it were coming from a thousand miles away, "but somehow I knew you'd be here."

I looked up as she sat next to me—having put on a jacket like myself—and looked out at the sea, which crashed and breathed. "You always were more thoughtful than you let on," she said. She leaned into me with surprising intimacy. "More dutiful, more decent. It was the first thing I noticed about you."

I didn't say anything, only gazed out at the water and the swirling pterodactyls—one of which glided in for a landing.

At last she said: "It doesn't have to be this way, you know. We could pretend we never came here ... that nothing ever happened—even go our separate ways, if that's what you want."

I looked at my shoes—the ones I'd found at Walmart—and tried to smile. "You'd just come back. Back here, I mean. It—I think it's a part of you now. Part of your makeup."

Neither of us said anything as the birds squawked and wheeled and the sun sank toward the sea.

"Maybe. But does it matter? You'd be long gone. And who knows, maybe I can learn something from them. Something that ..." She trailed off; her face suddenly ashen.

"I'm sorry," I said, and gripped the gun. "But I—I can't let you do it. And I think we both know why."

She looked at me somewhat blankly before getting up slowly and walking to the edge of the breaker. "And so you're just going to casually blow me away, is that it? Just air me out, as they say?" She laughed, but when she turned to face me her eyes were full of compassion, not malice. "And you think you can really do that? Just whiff me out like a match?" She shook her head. "No you can't, Francis. I know you better than that—or I'd never come with you in the first place. Please. Put down the gun. You're not a murderer. Not even they could turn you into one. You know that."

I stood but kept the pistol trained on her, moving toward her slowly, closing the gap between us. "I'm not just going to stand by while you—while you kill the people of Barley. I—I'll never do that, Amelia. I'm sorry. And if that means ... If that means—"

"Shhh," she said. "Listen to yourself." She held her hand out between us. "Give me the gun, Francis. Please. You don't want to do this, I know. Give it to me."

I shook my head, trying to resist. There was something about her now; something about her eyes. Just a hint of strange color—a hint of *them*—which made them oddly hypnotic, oddly compelling. "I don't—I can't—"

And then she leapt forward—suddenly, violently— snatching the gun from my hand, shoving me from the rock—*hard*—turning it on me even as I got to my feet—my head bleeding from the fall.

"Well now—how the times change." She cocked the weapon decisively. "And to think it wanted me to kill you and I refused!"

I raised my hands even while avoiding her eyes. "Now, just—settle down, okay? Nobody's going to kill anybody. All right?" I took a step backward—focusing on the gun, on its 9mm barrel. "I mean, we're two for two—right? I spared you ... and now, hopefully, you'll spare me."

She didn't respond, only continued sighting me, her lower lip trembling.

At last she said, "It's crazy, isn't it? Pointing guns at each other—as though we've somehow been enemies and not friends." Her eyes began to well up markedly, profusely. *"I've never wanted to hurt you, Francis.* But you have to understand, that—I'm no longer alone. That there's something else inside me now, and that it's vying—"

I stepped forward suddenly and she jerked the gun to track me.

"It's all right," I said. "It's all right. It's just that—"

And that's when it happened: that's when the silver and black plesiosaur breached the water like a mirage—its needle-teeth flashing and its dark neck glistening; its great flippers raked back like the wings of a plane—and snatched her from the rocks as though she were a doll. That's when the two of them seemed to hang briefly in the air—painted redden gold and burnt orange by the sun; rendered exquisite for a single fleeting instant—before crashing back to sea with a mighty smack and spray—and vanishing completely in its rough, roiling waters.

By the time I headed out the next day, the sun was at 12 o'clock and I'd fashioned two markers—one for the keeper and one for Amelia—both of which I'd planted atop breakers so they wouldn't be swept away. And then I'd made a sign—a sign for future travelers—which I'd hemmed and hawed over considerably before finally scrawling across it: GO TO BARLEY HOT SPRINGS IN MONTANA. STAY AWAY FROM THE LANTERN. Nor was it lost on me that the strange anomaly—who's very purpose had been to perpetuate the Flashback and thus usher men from the earth—would now be used to connect us; and to offer survivors hope. And I supposed that in the Big Empty, that was as good as it got.

And then I was off—having locked the tower door and disposed of its key—driving through Charleston and Barview and Coos Bay, following Tremont Avenue until it merged with Route 101, driving the Oregon Coast Highway all the way to Tillamook and beyond.

THE EYES OF ABYSS

Bridger Cummings

Captain Logan Petrov read his daily report for Mission Control of Helix-Aug on Earth on his tablet. If management on Earth did not get their daily report, they would of course bring it up at his next performance review as an excuse to not give him a raise yet again. This had not been a good day. Carlos had almost dropped an entire pallet of carbon panels on Jennifer, and she reacted by yelling at him, walking off, and refusing to do any actual work for the rest of her shift. Carlos claimed it was because the sun was in his eyes, which should be expected on Mercury. Regardless, Andrew and Carlos managed to do a lot of the planned work before Jennifer finally returned from her walk on the surface of the barren planet, where they were installing an outpost. The three of them flew the shuttle back up to their cruiser, parked at the L2 Lagrange point behind Mercury. This shielded them from the Sun, which they did not need power from since their ship had a nuclear reactor. It was another delay for their already strapped crew, and he hesitated to send the bad news. They were drastically behind schedule. But if he did not, MC would be displeased. And when mission control was not happy, the threats resumed. He sent off the report.

If he did not strap himself in to the bed on the spaceship's zero-G, he would float away and bump into the walls. Looking to his side, Logan smiled at the photo of his family—his wife, their daughter, and himself—and composed a message for them. It had been several days since his last message, and it annoyed him that he talked with MC more than his wife. He told them how much he missed them and that it would only be another two months before he would be done with this mission of building the initial Mercury outpost. He reminded his wife, unnecessarily, about her upcoming doctor's visit for the quarterly treatment. That was the entire reason he had this job anyway. He stressed how much he loved them and sent it off before going to sleep.

The next morning, Andrew, Carlos, and this time Liu left for Mercury from the *SC Nebula* with more construction supplies. Logan had just seen them off and went up to the bridge. He pushed off the entryway, floating through the air, and reached the communications terminal to see the transmission flagged as *High Priority*. He did not expect any official communication for a couple of weeks. This meant business.

June 12, 2072 11:41 ECT

SC Nebula and Captain Petrov

An unexpected solar flare and coronal mass ejection hit the International Space Station Venus. *We cannot establish any communication since the event yesterday. The* Space Cruiser Nebula *is the closest available ship that could investigate ASAP. This is an emergency, and you are to abandon your current construction mission and depart immediately. Ascertain the situation, and assist as necessary. We will continue our attempts to contact the* ISS Venus *while you are enroute and provide further instructions. Regardless of the outcome, your current assignment will be considered complete and paid fully once you return to Earth.*

Jennifer poked her head into the bridge, her blonde braid swinging behind her. "Moin, Logan," she called out, interrupting the constant hum of the air scrubbers. "What's up?"

Logan turned around, holding onto a rail beside to the terminal. He wore a blue standard-issue jumper from their company.

"High-priority message from MC." Logan rubbed his hand over his shaved head, feeling his rough stubbles. "The Venus station's been hit by a flare, and it's radio silent. We're the lucky ship that can get there the fastest, so we're leaving now."

Jennifer raised an eyebrow, creasing her weathered forehead. "Now?" Her self-consciousness regarding her French caused her to speak little.

"Immediately. We need to recall Andrew before they make it planet side."

The front half of the *Nebula* housed the living quarters. The back half was a giant cargo bay that held all the prefabricated panels and other supplies for the outpost. It could be pressurized, but it usually was not. At the rear end was the reactor and engines. Halfway along the ship was a shuttle bay, with a door opening to space on the starboard side. Airlocks surrounded the shuttle bay. Opposite the shuttle bay, on the port side of the ship, was the locker room, which held the EVA suits and had a telescoping docking tube for connecting to other ships.

Andrew and Jennifer waited behind the airlock and watched as Andrew navigated the shuttle into its bay. The gaping door to the exterior slid closed like a barn door as the docking clamps grasped the shuttle. The room pressurized, indicated by a green light by Logan. He opened the airlock as the shuttle's door opened. Out glided Carlos followed by Liu.

"Hey Boss," Carlos grinned. "Long time no see, eh?" He had short, black hair and dark skin and was the tallest member of the crew by at least a foot. He and Jennifer were the engineers who ensured the outpost was constructed properly, even though everyone had to work on it.

Liu, the ship's doctor, grabbed a bar on the outside of the shuttle. "This must be urgent. What's up?" She was short, thin, and muscular, and she always wore shorts and a t-shirt, which afforded her maximum comfort. She liked to leave her hair loose, and her fine, black hair fanned out like an aura

"Yeah, something like that," Logan rapped his fingers on a handrail while waiting for Andrew, who came out after he had completely shut off the shuttle.

Andrew was short with buzzed, dark hair and a pale face that always looked like he squinted at some imagined sun. He preferred to wear a blue jumper, like Logan.

After waiting for Andrew, since Logan hated explaining himself twice, he told them about the change in their mission.

As the ships primary pilot, Andrew realized why at first. "This is because Earth is on the other side of the Sun, isn't it?"

Mercury and Venus were relatively close together, in conjunction on the other side of the sun from the Earth.

Logan nodded. "Correct. We just happen to be in the wrong place at the wrong time. We're the closest free ship."

"This damn war..." Carlos grumbled.

Jennifer grunted in agreement.

"I know," Logan frowned. "But since Mars is so close to Earth right now, most civilian ships are being drafted to resupply the blockade. We need to leave before we pass Venus. But the good thing is that once we go there, we can go straight back to Earth with full pay, shaving months off our current job."

He winked at Liu, who was often vocal about retiring as soon as possible even though she was only in her late thirties.

That improved the mood, and the five of them set about locking down anything not bolted down and preparing for the three-week flight to Venus.

The five of them gathered on the bridge, which was at the front of the ship with windows offering a sweeping view of the stars. Logan stole a glance at the eclipse caused by Mercury. They had been here for a month, and they had two more to go. But the outpost would have to wait.

Andrew required a few minutes planning their flight path on the computer while the others chatted. Liu wanted to retire as soon as she could while Carlos was saving up to go back to college, and they both professed their choice to be the better one.

Andrew entered the final command. The thrusters lit up on the long, cylindrical *SC Nebula*, and the crew were pushed to the back of their seats.

"Was nice while it lasted. . ." Jennifer mumbled in her thick accent.

Carlos laughed. "Yeah, but I'm looking forward to playing some more poker on the way there." He raised his voice for effect. "I hope you're looking forward to losing another couple hundred bucks, Andrew!"

"Screw you, man!" Andrew shouted back. "If anything, I'll clean Logan out and get that bottle of booze he's hoarding."

Logan could not help grinning. "Negative. I already told you, that bottle will be the first bottle of Scotch to go to Mercury and back, and it's for Nina." Both Logan and his wife enjoyed sipping on whiskey, and this would be the first bottle to get that close to the Sun.

The others laughed and discussion returned to their normal banter.

Logan's mind dwelled on his family. He thought of Nina and their daughter, Amy. *I hope I can get home early to see them sooner.*

Logan heard back from his wife about ten days later—about halfway to Venus. Her infusion had gone well, and she felt revitalized. She decided to take Amy out to the mountains for a simple walk. "Thank you so much Logan," her message went. "I love you, and I can't thank you enough for all that you sacrifice for our family, and for me. Come home safe, my love."

His face warmed after reading her message. It was the one reprieve from the monotony of traveling through space. The only reason he had taken this job in the first place was because Helix-Aug was one of the few companies in the world that covered his wife's medical condition under its insurance plan. Logan had started off in security for the company, but his organization and willingness to carry out corporate directives saw him rapidly promoted to new positions until he ended up being captain of one of the cargo ships.

It was time for the crew's weekly training, so he unclipped himself from his bed and looked for the others. He overheard Carlos in the mess hall.

"Did you hear some more ships defected to the rebellion?"

Andrew snorted. "It's all propaganda. The Martians will grab at any straw that gives them legitimacy."

"I dunno. They seem to often get the short end of the stick. What's your beef with Mars anyway?"

"It's not Mars itself. It's the rebels. I used to fly between Earth and Mars. I helped build some of the first outposts. And now that I and others did that, they want to break off from the Union. It pisses me off."

"Well, I guess I can see your point. But I still think ships are defecting."

Andrew smirked. "Wanna bet on it?"

"Sure! Fifty bucks says it's true."

Andrew laughed. "You're on. And when we—" He stopped when Logan pulled himself into the room.

Logan looked between them. "You know we're not supposed to talk about that."

Andrew's toes hooked under a bar to hold himself in position. "Well, Jen's not here, right?"

"The problem is if she did come around, she could have heard you all the way from down the hall. Like I just did."

"Sorry, Boss." Carlos said. "Do you know how her brother, Thomas, has been?"

"Last I heard, he was fine. But that was a week ago or so when Jen mentioned it. Not a lot gets past the jammers around Mars."

Andrew grunted. "Seriously, this rebellion is pulling all the ships out and leaving with us with nothing but a skeleton crew. It sucks. And then innocent people like Thomas get caught in the middle of it."

"I know," Logan responded. "But be glad that we weren't pulled in to support the blockade either. At least we are doing something elsewhere. Nothing worse than shuffling around Mars and hoping you don't get hit with one of their," Logan made air quotes "'warning' missiles."

They all chuckled, but everyone forced it. The news about ships defecting was not proven, but the Union would not admit to their own ships getting attacked unless it were true. And Helix-Aug tried to stay in the black while dealing with mandated Union assignments.

"Let's go and find the others," Logan said. "We've got to get our weekly training in. Only about another week until we get to the Venus station."

An amber glow flooded the bridge through the windows and viewing ports.

"Visual contact with the station established," Andrew announced over the intercom.

It didn't take long for Logan to pull himself into the bridge and clip himself into his seat. "Put it on the screen." *Why aren't they responding?* They had been making hourly short-range radio attempts, but they may have been alone in this sector for all the response they got.

Carlos and Liu held onto handholds next to portholes near the bridge, gazing at Venus. Jennifer came onto the bridge shortly after Logan and got in her own seat.

Andrew touched a couple of buttons for the central screen to display a camera feed.

Logan squinted at the magnified screen. A thin, white T-shape floated in space at the periphery of Venus, illuminated from the right with a yellowish radiance from the swirling clouds of the planet.

"Lights are still on. . ." Jennifer mumbled.

Logan peered into the distance before looking back at the screen. The top half of the station's exterior lights flashed. "Indeed, but it might mean nothing. Andrew, open communication on all channels again. Maximum strength." He waited for Andrew. "Attention *ISS Venus*, this is the *SC Nebula.* Do you copy? Over." He waited a minute before trying again as the crew waited in silence. "Attention *ISS Venus*, this is the *SC Nebula.* Do you copy? Over."

Silence.

"Prepare a transmission to MC," Logan said. "I think we'll be talking more than once a day now." He waited until Andrew was ready. "Mission Control, this is Captain Logan Petrov of the *SC Nebula.* We have visual contact with the *ISS Venus.* The station is still powered and the lights are on. Repeat, lights are still on, but there is no radio response. Requesting permission to board and investigate. Over."

Andrew dispatched the message, and an electric silence filled the bridge while they waited the eight minutes it would take for a response. The station slowly grew as their ship approached it.

"ETA to the station?" Logan asked.

Andrew checked the dashboard. "About an hour at this rate. Hopefully we got here fast enough . . . "

"I hope so," is what Logan said, but *it's likely a bunch of corpses* is what he thought. "Let's wait until MC contacts us—" and as if on cue, the dashboard showed a message from Mission Control. Andrew played it.

"Captain Petrov, this is Venus Station lead James Anderson at Mission Control. Fly around the station and check for any potential dangers. There should be three other cargo ships docked at the station. After determining it to be safe, you have permission to enter the station. Notify MC immediately if anything changes. Otherwise, we will monitor the live feed, with a four-minute delay, of course. Over."

"Understood, James. Proceeding to station now." Logan looked from the window to his right to find Andrew staring at him. "You heard him. Fly in between the station and the planet and maintain a distance of about two hundred meters." Logan looked back at Jennifer behind him. "Keep all cameras fixed on the station. I want everyone looking at that screen or out a viewing port for anything odd."

"We are within desired range of the station," Andrew announced. "Going to fly around the station now."

Thousands of carbon-composite plates of varying shades of white and gray comprised the *ISS Venus*. The frame resembled a giant "T" with the upper half revolving around the axis so the two arms and upper section of the cylinder could spin to create artificial gravity. Andrew thought of his daughter, spinning around during ballet class with her arms outstretched. It seemed like a lonely dancer, with all of Venus as its stage.

The station had been built eight years ago by the Union, but it was currently leased out by a joint venture from Helix-Aug and Lightscreen Inc, which is why the former called upon Logan's ship. The base of the T housed the loading bay and science lab, where the two companies worked on various projects, at the opposite end from the arms. Some ships were docked at the base of the station, which offered no lighting.

"The bottom half is dark," Carlos said.

Andrew spoke to nobody in particular, "I guess the *whole* station isn't powered."

Liu considered that. "Shouldn't the emergency power route through the entire station?"

Logan's eyes didn't leave the screen as he responded. "Like our ship, it has a nuclear reactor, so it's not like they ran out of power. Unless maybe some parts failed?"

"A meltdown?" Liu asked.

"No, the station has a fusion plant. Maybe there was a catastrophic failure because of the flare? Maybe the bottom part depressurized, so they decided not to waste energy there?"

Andrew wasn't sure about that. "Shouldn't the reactor provide more than they would ever need?"

Logan frowned. "Right now, we all know as much as anyone else. We won't know for sure until we go in."

Andrew looked at the radar. "In any case, I can't detect any of the station's gas-harvesting drones. It's just us and the station."

After a few more minutes of flying by the station, Jennifer spoke up. "I only see two docked ships."

Andrew glanced at another monitor. "This station has four docking ports, but James and the flight logs say three ships should be docked. Can anyone see a third?"

She continued looking as their ship finished its orbit around the station. "No. Only two ships docked."

Liu and Carlos added their support of that observation from their viewing ports.

Logan grunted. *Where was the third ship?*

"What do you think, Logan?" Andrew asked.

"We can't get use the shuttle, can we?"

"Nope. Not without them opening their shuttle door."

"Understood." Logan rubbed his stubbly head while he pondered. "We'll have to manually bypass the airlock if the power is out, but I'd rather use the docking ports than trying to enter through an emergency hatch. Bring the ship in to docking port four."

"You got it." Andrew adjusted their heading and started their approach.

The enormous *SC Nebula* needed enough room and storage to stay in space for months at a time while hauling materials to build an outpost to Mercury, but the imposing size of the *ISS Venus* made their ship look like an ant in comparison. Docking the ship without the automated docking procedure linking with the station was tricky, but Andrew proved his worth. He used the side camera to bring the docking tube closer to the station's docking port, and with a mild jar as metal briefly scraped on metal after several minutes of fine tuning their approach, he sighed in relief.

"Docking successful," Andrew declared as he flicked a switch and the locking clamps at the end of the extended docking tube grappled the station.

Logan unbuckled himself. "Carlos and Liu, we're going in. Meet me in the locker room." He rose from his seat and turned around. "Jennifer, suit up as well, and stay on board in case we need assistance. Andrew, I want you to stay on comms here in the *Nebula*. Keep pinging the station."

"Sure thing," Andrew said.

Jennifer nodded.

The other two pushed off toward the locker room.

The four donned their suits in silence while they listened to Andrew periodically calling out to the station over the radio. The hollow rustle of clothing sent a shiver down Logan's spine. He didn't usually get intimidated, but it's not every day you break into a radio-silent space station.

After they all got dressed into the white spacesuits with blue accents, they checked the seals and made sure everyone was tethered, in case the tube broke while they were in it. Logan and Carlos held laser cutters usually used for cutting pipes while Liu clutched her medkit, even though all the tools were tethered to their suits.

In her own EVA suit, Jennifer hovered by the control terminal.

Logan looked at the airlock while testing the radio. "Andrew, you there?"

"Loud and clear, Captain."

"Good. We're going in." He nodded to Jennifer.

Carlos opened the door of the airlock followed by Logan and Liu. With three people in the airlock, it was difficult to turn around, so Jennifer closed the door behind them. The pressure in the cramped airlock lowered to match the vacuum of the docking tube between the *SC Nebula* and the *ISS Venus*.

Carlos opened the outer door and they were all briefly blinded by the amber light that flooded in from the windows going along the docking tube. Once Carlos put his hand down from blocking the light, he propelled himself through the tube and grabbed onto the station. He fiddled with the controls on the station for a few seconds.

"It's not going to open, Boss. The external door's lock won't release without power."

"Pressure on the other side?"

Carlos put his faceplate against the tiny porthole on the airlock, looking for the physical pressure gauge. It was in a different location than on their ship, so it took him a moment of casting his headlamp around before he located it. "Looks about zero."

Logan nodded. "Well, that's what we brought the cutters for."

"You sure, Boss?"

He considered for a moment. "Do it. If we wait for MC to respond, they will tell us to do this anyway. It's not like we could get in through an emergency hatch without cutting it open either. We could repair the hatch someday, if necessary."

"Whatever you say, Boss." Carlos fired up his laser, filling the tube with a reddish glow that meshed warmly with the yellow glow of Venus. A few minutes passed, and the door swung outward as the laser severed the bolt. The trio entered the station's airlock. After ensuring there was no pressure on the other said, inside the station, Carlos yanked a lever and pushed the inner door open.

Liu spoke up. "No pressure. . . Maybe there's air farther in the station."

"Maybe." Logan had his doubts. "Let's go in and find out."

The three entered the loading bay. Their helmet-mounted lights cast sharp white spotlights in front of them, and a pale glow of yellow creeped in from the few windows and the open airlock. Logan started when Carlos shouted in surprise. Somebody floated toward Carlos.

Not a person. A corpse.

The shadows kept secret many of the details. But it was clear that the corpse did not have a helmet on. And Logan thought he saw something else. He told everyone to look for the control panel. With the ship connected to the station, like jump starting a car, they power-cycled the panel to breathe some life into this part of the station. The station hummed, and the lights flickered on.

They looked around, but the corpse demanded their attention as it spun its deathly waltz. What Logan had at first attributed to the poor lighting, he now saw as reality. Small growths protruded sporadically from his skin, like fingers poking out of his limbs and torso. They were the same shade as the rest of his skin, and Logan imagined something inside the skin trying to escape by pushing outward like an insect. The corpse wore only the lower part of a pressure suit. It looked like he could only get so far before running out of air, leaving him partially mummified after the exposure to the vacuum of space with his mouth open in a perpetual scream. Even with his EVA suit on, Logan did not want to touch the corpse. Andrew's voice on the radio interrupted his brooding.

"Everything all right? Looks like the lights are back on. Is that a body I see on your feed?"

“Indeed. . . Andrew, we've found a corpse. It looks like he got his pressure suit only halfway on before asphyxiating. We're going to try and get into the science lab now.”

“Understood. Also, James doesn’t know about the missing third ship. No flight plans exist.”

“Not good. And there are weird things growing on the corpse.”

“Growing?”

“Kind of like a potato when it grows eyes. I count about a dozen, and they're all about the size of a finger and look skin-colored as well.”

“Oookaay. . . Hard to make out any growths in the video. I'll tell James.”

“Carlos, try to access the terminal and find out what happened,” Logan said. He turned to Liu, a natural thing to do regardless of their radios. “Let's check out the science lab.”

Past the loading bay lay the science lab, followed by the gardens, where residents grew and stored food. The science lab did not spin, so zero-G testing could be done, as well as the loading area to facilitate smooth docking. An actuator assembly with gyro stabilization housed the airlock between the science bay and gardens, so the upper half of the station could rotate. Beyond the garden, at the junction of the two arms, lay a small viewing Cupola. One arm of the station housed the living area and command center. The other arm housed the power supply and the gas harvesting processor that sent out drones to extract a rare and valuable gas composite found in the Venusian atmosphere.

Logan turned and kicked off toward the airlock with Liu close behind. He grasped the handle of the airlock and looked through the porthole.

“See anything?” Liu asked while trying to see over his shoulder.

“Negative. I can see into the airlock, but I can't see through the other window for some reason. Looks blocked.”

Carlos spoke up. "Boss, it appears the SRR has been manually shut off and locked. I can't override it."

"Odd. Why did they shut off their radio?" Logan wondered out loud. "Anything about the missing ship?"

He typed in a few commands. "Not much. It shows that it departed for an unscheduled trip eighteen days ago, but that's it. No further data."

Logan looked back as Liu voiced her concern. "There is pressure on the other side of the door, and this airlock is big enough for only one person at a time."

"Yes," Logan said, "and I'll go in first." He powered up his laser cutter momentarily to make sure it worked before turning it off again.

Carlos joined them at the airlock. "You sure, Boss?"

Logan brushed off their objections and stepped into the airlock, closing the door behind him. Pushing the controls, he waited for the tiny cavity to fill with air. A light on the other door turned green, and he slowly opened the door into the science lab. Logan expected to see more corpses floating in stale air, the victims of a rescue come too late. But spaced out around the door were three people. Like the first corpse, they all had several growths reminiscent of potato eyes protruding off their skin, but theirs were all several inches thick and about a foot along. They looked like leafless trees dwarfing over him. Logan briefly remembered camping in the fall and looking up at the night sky between the limbs of trees that had shed their leaves.

One of them, with two growths on her head like horns, repositioned herself. And it looked like she held a piece of pipe with her other hand like a club.

"Whoa!" Logan shouted in a muffle through his suit, instinctively throwing up his free hand.

Rooted in place, Logan could only watch her swing the pipe in seemingly slow motion. One of the other protrusion-infested survivors let go of his club and whipped his free hand around and stopped her arm right before hitting Logan. Logan's savior was even more fearsome, with a long, fleshy growth protruding directly from his throat.

"What are you doing?" the horned-growth mutant shrieked at the other as she tried pushing the club the last few inches to Logan's chest. She glared at Logan with murder in her eyes.

Through his space suit, Logan could barely hear them. *Should have turned on the external mics,* Logan thought to himself.

The one with the horn-like growths appeared middle-aged, and her pale skin was taut, like the other two mutants. The one who stopped her appeared to be in his fifties, and he took deep, pained breaths due to a growth on his neck. The third deformed survivor was younger and held onto the doorway. He seemed unsure of himself, looking between Logan and his two companions with his one eye—a growth on his right temple blocked that eye. Fleshy limbs grew on all three of them—a couple dozen long branches of grisly protrusions. What little hair they had left was thin and sparse. Their loose and tattered clothes had holes cut out where these things stuck out from their bodies and grew outward. With a few growths protruding from each limb and around eight or nine on their torsos, Logan thought they looked like a haunted forest.

"He's not one of them!" the older one wheezed. "Look at him!"

She relaxed her arm and looked between him and Logan. Every movement jostled the growths on her body, like stalks of wheat blowing in the wind.

What happened to them?

Meanwhile, Carlos and Liu watched the standoff through the porthole, and Logan's radio cackled nonstop.

"What's happening?!"

"Do you need help?"

"We're going to cut open this door!"

Andrew's confused voice joined the fray. "What's going on? I can't see anything on the video."

Logan straightened his back and filled his lungs. "Everyone be quiet!" He activated his external speaker and microphone. "My name is Captain Logan Petrov. I am with the *SC Nebula* from Helix-Aug, and MC sent us here after the station went silent. What's going on?"

The three in front of Logan exchanged furtive glances, their growths swaying in the non-existent breeze.

The older one turned toward Logan and croaked, "You shouldn't have come."

"We came to help. . ." Logan's mouth opened and closed a few times, unsure what more to say.

The female survivor's shoulders slumped, and Logan could see tears pooling in her eyes. She maneuvered her arm past a growth coming out of her chest to wipe the tears away.

The older one patted her back and took a labored breath before looking intently at Logan. "My name is David. The flare threw everything out of whack."

"You the only survivors?"

David looked at the other two. His voice quavered, and Logan leaned forward to understand him. "No, but it's complicated." David followed Logan's stare toward the growth protruding from his neck. He laughed hollowly while frowning. "Yeah, something is wrong with us. There's a lot to explain. Let's go into the garden." He pointed toward the back of the lab.

Liu wanted to come through at once to check out their condition.

Carlos was not as sure. "They look a little messed up, don't you think, Boss?"

Liu, having already passed through the airlock, yelled back, "Carlos, they need help. That's what we came here to do. Get your butt through here while we figure this out."

Carlos was not happy to oblige, but he finally did and came through the airlock too.

The six of them floated through the science lab to the gardens, careful not to touch anything. What was once a clean, white lab was now splattered with stains. Bags filled with browns and yellows—human refuse—were anchored to the walls, and they had to take care not to collide with them. A bloody bag in one corner held bones with the meat picked too clean. Logan exchanged glances with Liu, who arched an eyebrow. Logan casually placed his finger on the trigger of his laser cutter.

"Sorry about this," David indicated toward a couple of the bags while pulling himself along the handholds in the science lab. "We can't get to the normal toilets and had to improvise. It looks even worse now that you guys got the lights back on. . ." His face reddened as he looked away. Without saying anything more, he grabbed the handle on the airlock to the gardens.

With the air pressure equal on both sides, both doors opened freely. Although he had seen the growths on the other three, Logan's eyes still went wide when he saw the other four survivors inside the gardens.

One waited by the door they just opened, club in hand and standing on the ladder that led up to the airlock. Behind her, dirt lined the cylindrical wall with only a few meager stalks of pale vegetation growing. A refracting mirror system along the walls took in sunlight from the outside and dispersed it amongst the plants. The reflected light created an eerie underglow in the room, like when a child holds a flashlight under their face while telling scary stories. The station started revolving with the gardens to simulate a weak gravity in the upper half, and Logan briefly got vertigo looking down the cylinder.

The other three survivors in the gardens huddled up with clubs—pieces of pipe or loose shelves—at the far end of the garden section, guarding the opposite door. They turned to look.

After a quick introduction, the solitary guard in front of the party descended the ladder to the exterior wall, and the others followed, adjusting to the mild artificial gravity.

David introduced Logan to Kate, the *de facto* leader. Face white and taut, all her hair fallen out, around twenty of the foot-long growths stuck out of her body, and with a permanent grimace, she greeted Logan.

"As the VP of off-world research, Sascha Hudson was supposed to command this station," Logan said. "Did he pass away?"

"No, not exactly," she began, "he's still alive in fact." She continued at seeing Logan's eyes scan the room for Sascha. "Let me start from the beginning. The flare hit us with a strength we were not prepared for, and it overpowered our redundancies. Quite a few people in under-protected areas died from radiation sickness after only a few days. The lucky ones got cooked alive by microwaves immediately. Our systems went crazy, too, and we struggled to get them back online. The exposure killed most of the crops as well, as you can see." She waved her arm across the room.

Logan broke in, "But there should be plenty of prepared rations?"

"There is, but *Sascha* has them all." She sneered while saying his name. "He and a few others freaked out and barricaded themselves at the end of the station."

"What? Why?"

She sighed. "Things were crazy. People were dying from radiation sickness, and we tried to get the station running properly again after so many electronics failed. We had been working on getting one of the ships working so we could go back home, and *Sascha* chose a couple people to test it. We told him it wasn't ready yet!" She collected her thoughts. "Sammy and Michael went in. They disconnected from the station and were supposed to come right back, but something went wrong. They couldn't reactivate the thruster and got caught up in Venus's gravity. We could only watch as their ship got closer to the planet and was pulled in. As if watching your friends burn up in the clouds wasn't bad enough, we then started growing these, these things!" She touched a growth protruding from her stomach and winced at the contact.

Logan studied her and the others for a minute. "What happened?"

Kate closed her eyes and took a deep breath. "It started shortly after the flare. Maybe a few days. Rebecca started feeling itchy. At first, we thought it was radiation sickness. Then she started getting little bumps. It didn't take long for the bumps to grow out like you see on all of us. After a few days, the rest of us started feeling itchy too."

"Sounds like a contagion," Liu said. "We haven't opened our suits yet, and I get the feeling we shouldn't."

"Yeah, best we can tell, some gamma rays mutated some otherwise benign microbe in the station, turning it into this nightmare."

Carlos pointed at one of her protrusions. "Do they hurt?"

"Not so much. More uncomfortable, but they do get in the way sometimes."

"Why don't you cut them off?"

"Oh, some tried. There's definitely blood and nerves inside, so it hurts when you do that." She glared at her own body and the four growths jutting out from her chest and stomach, like giant fingers reaching out from her. "We feel hungry all the time. It's draining us like a parasite."

"If Sascha has all the rations, how did you manage to survive so long?"

"There are still some okay vegetables. . ." she trailed off and glanced at the door to the science lab.

Logan's heart beat a little faster.

Kate didn't say anything more.

After an extended pause, Logan lowered his voice. "I saw bones in the other room."

She looked down at the floor, refusing to meet his eyes. Her voice quavered. "We were so hungry. . . He was already dead. . ."

"I see."

"Please. . ." Kate's eyes snapped back up to meet Logan's as she whispered. "Help us."

"We're here to help, but I need to talk to MC first."

Logan relayed a message to James. In the meantime, Jennifer and Carlos brought in some food rations, which the survivors devoured. While the others ate, Logan questioned Kate further.

"This still doesn't explain why Sascha locked himself away from you guys."

"Right." She stopped eating but kept glancing at the food while licking her lips. "*Sascha* and a few of the managers decided Sammy and Michael would test the ship. After they died, Sammy's husband accused Sascha of murder. A little extreme, but emotions were running high. Then everyone started getting these growths. Sascha freaked out. He and the rest of the R&D team haven't come out in more than two weeks. Honestly, I wonder if he's somehow responsible for all of this." She looked at the other survivors. "He was always coy about his research."

"How many of them are in there?"

"Four, including *Sascha*."

"Why are the other researchers not stopping him?"

"Well, all four of them decided on the two that would test the ship. They are all seniors in Lightscreen. Maybe it's a joint guilt?"

Logan counted. *Seven survivors in this room and four in the other room. Only eleven remaining from the full crew of thirty-four.* His thoughts returned to Sascha. "But you outnumber them? You couldn't overwhelm them?"

Kate lightly rolled her eyes. "Logan, most of us are scientists. We're not soldiers. Their decision took us by surprise, and they barricaded themselves past the door out of the gardens. We tried to get in a few days after they first locked themselves in, but they created some gun-like thing that launches spikes. Engineers, huh? Someone is always manning it, and it's aimed right at the door. They already got a couple of us. . ." She glanced at the door of the lab then back to Logan.

"Couldn't you fix the other two ships?"

"We can't get into the spacesuits anymore!" She spread her arms and looked down at her body, indicating the root-like growths protruding from her body and torn-up clothing.

"Right," he muttered, "sorry about that."

"We tried it once, actually. The air pump in the loading bay failed a few days after we lost Sammy and Michael, but Aaron volunteered to try getting into his spacesuit to repair another ship. When he never returned, we assumed the worst."

"We came upon a corpse in the loading bay. His suit was only halfway on."

"Then I guess you found him. . ."

"And no SOS calls?"

"We tried fixing the radio, but we didn't manage before *Sascha* locked himself in where it's located."

Logan nodded. "We saw the communications were functioning, but deactivated."

"That bastard! He must have fixed it but then deactivated it. He's gone crazy, I tell you."

"If what you say is true, I'm surprised he hasn't investigated our arrival."

"We were also surprised, but I guess he saw your ship with the camera system. We felt the station jolt a little, and that's why the others waited by the doors. We feared Sascha went around and intended to attack us. We honestly just don't know what he's up to anymore."

They grew quiet, and Kate took the opportunity to swallow mouthfuls of her meal. Logan listened to a transmission from James and lowered his voice to relay a message back. While waiting for an answer, he continued talking to Kate while Liu inspected the seven survivors. The orders came in. The main branch of Helix-Aug R&D wanted to bring the research to a station in orbit around Earth. Undoubtably, it would be worth a small fortune if they could figure out what was going on and sell it to the Union. James told Logan that if he didn't get the research and the people involved, then they might take his wife's condition off the list of covered illnesses on the company health insurance policy. This was how Helix-Aug repeatedly got Logan to do whatever they wanted.

Logan raised his voice. "Orders from MC. We are to evacuate the station and bring everyone with us and all the data on the research here. Corporate wants it all. Jennifer, Liu, and Andrew, pressurize and prepare the cargo hold for the survivors." Whispering, so only those on their ship's radio channel could hear, Logan added, "And isolate the entryway. We don't want to infect the entire ship if this is airborne."

Jennifer spoke up. "But what if they get us sick? What if I take it back home to my daughter?"

Carlos chimed in. "I agree, Boss. This doesn't sound like a good idea."

"We have our orders. And you all know that I can't say no. . . We have to take everyone and everything involved, and we'll do our best to keep them quarantined." His voice softened. "I also have a daughter, Jennifer. I don't want her getting infected any more than you do yours."

As everyone started moving around, Kate spoke up. "We can't get through the docking bay without air."

"We got the power running again. Andrew, what can you come up with?"

"Let me work on it. We can likely flood the docking bay with air from our ship."

Logan paused, considering the doors they had cut open and how the ship and station would share air. "Okay, get on it, but make sure the path is isolated. Carlos, you're with me." He turned to the survivors. "David, I need you and a few others. It's time for us to talk to Sascha."

Logan led Carlos, David, and two other survivor-volunteers to the airlock between the garden and the junction. The other survivors were already in the *SC Nebula.*

"Careful," David wheezed. "Some sort of spike gun."

Logan nodded, opened the first airlock, and knocked on the second door. He waited a minute before knocking again, and, barely perceptible through the door and his spacesuit, Logan heard someone on the other side.

"Go away!"

Logan grumbled about them not using a radio. He shouted to introduce himself over his suit's external speaker and demanded to talk to Sascha. A moment's silence, and then another voice.

"This is Sascha."

"We're here to bring everyone and all the research back to Earth to a secure station. That includes you guys. Unlock this door."

"Just take the others and go."

Logan looked back at the others briefly and shook his head. "Don't you want to go home? Unlock the door and bring your research, and this can go smoothly."

Silence.

"He's not complying," Logan said into his headset. "Jennifer and Liu, prepare a restraint system in the cargo hold. I think we'll have to bring in a few of them by force." He turned to Carlos. "Cut open the door."

Carlos turned on his cutter and started cutting around the locking arm. After a few minutes, he moved to the side, nodding at Logan. Logan tried pushing the door. It didn't initially budge, and Logan braced himself to push with his feet. The door squeaked and moved a little bit before getting stuck again. Through the narrow opening, he could see boxes and bits of metal frames.

"They barricaded the door a while ago," one of the survivors said.

Logan forced the door open a little bit more. "Sascha, come with us! Get this junk out of the way!"

They heard a loud bang as a metal spike bounced off the doorframe.

Sascha shouted, "just take the others and leave! I can't let either of our companies get a hold of this research!"

I do not care about your research and wish I could leave you, but my wife's more important. Logan turned to the others. "He's not coming peacefully. We need to clear out the barricade and get them."

Logan waited until Jennifer radioed that she was in position, and he gave the go-ahead. From outside, she punctured the hull of the station near the junction, only big enough to cause a pressure loss as the air rushed to escape into space. A gust flowed through the chamber, and Logan could hear the debris behind the door shifting. He and Carlos pushed on the door, and their effort along with the rush of air gave them enough room to get inside the junction of the station. Logan and Carlos held metal plates in front of them like shields. Metal hit the barricade as the two plowed ahead and pushed debris out of the way. A couple loud clangs pierced their ears as spikes hammered them. The spike launcher could shoot much quicker than they expected, and it pelted their shields like hail.

As Logan and Carlos advanced, Logan could finally see the four renegades: one manning the turret, one nearby with spare spikes to load into the turret, and the other two standing near the corners of the station arms with makeshift clubs in hand. They were pale, haggard, and peppered with the same protrusions as the other survivors, breaching the rips in their dirty clothes. Logan reached the turret and used his laser cutter on the turret and, inadvertently, the operator's hands, instantly scorching one hand off. The operator recoiled, grabbing his stump and screeching in pain. The ammo holder and nearest club wielder hesitated upon seeing Logan orientate toward them.

"Drop your weapons!" Logan commanded, the glow of his laser tool illuminating him as a foreboding silhouette.

Logan glanced to the side. Carlos had blasted a crater in the chest of the fourth rebel with his laser cutter, killing him immediately. But Logan noticed a bubble of blood forming where a spike impaled Carlos's gut through his spacesuit.

Logan turned his attention to the three in front of him barely in time to see a club coming at him. Logan almost got his shield up, but the club connected with that arm, and pain flared and tears clouded his vision. He lashed out with his cutter. Logan heard a scream, and he hoped it came from his assailant.

Logan could barely focus on the people shuffling past him, his vision darkened by the pain in his arm. David and the other two followed Logan and Carlos and restrained the ones resisting. Once everyone was secure, one of the survivors patched the hole Jennifer made with emergency gel to stop the rush of air flying out the station.

David gently shook Logan. "You all right?"

Logan tried to focus. Everything was blurry with the pale, yellow light of Venus washing in through the Copula. "I dunno. Hurts so bad." He looked at his left forearm bent at an unnatural angle. "Did we get them?" he managed.

"Yeah, and the other one that's still alive. But Carlos. . ."

Logan struggled to clear his eyes and looked around for Carlos. He spotted Carlos sprawled and the growing pool of blood from his suit. "Liu, we need you!" His vision faded, and he lost consciousness.

The *SC Nebula* drifted toward Earth, having left Venus and the station a few days prior. Venus was now barely bigger than any of the stars scattered across the blanket of space.

Logan felt better and wanted to finally open a comms conversation with Sascha, who was locked into a fabricated room they built up in the cargo hold.

"We were scared." Sascha explained. "We were afraid of testing the ship ourselves, so we sent some low-level engineers. After it crashed into Venus, we thought we would get charged with negligent homicide."

"I don't think so. It didn't look good, but now you've committed much worse. You let many people starve and even killed a few in your fervor to isolate yourself."

"I. . ." he choked on his words. "We tried to contain the situation, but when we started getting infected, we knew it was over."

"What do you mean 'over?' Your job was to command the station. To stay cool in the face of danger. Instead, you made everything worse and starved the others."

"We all should have died. The research should be trashed." Sascha went quiet, and Logan was about to ask if he was still there when Sascha cleared his throat. "Do you even know what our companies were researching? Do you know why this station was one of the few still operational in the face of the rebellion? When most stations have been put in standby and almost all civilian ships are being drafted for the blockade, we're still out here. The Union military branch contracted our joint venture to create a new bioweapon. The gas composite here in Venus is a perfect catalyst for their desired weapon. One based off a fungi and that would manage to skirt the law. I purposely stalled development and tried to keep Lightscreen and Helix-Aug from getting a viable weapon to sell to the Union. Because what's going to happen if the Union gets something they could just flood the bio-domes on Mars with? Goodbye resistance. And now you will deliver everything right to Helix-Aug, who is taking everything. They'll see what we created and sell it to the Union."

"And you created this?"

"Well, me and my team did. But we had it isolated. It wasn't quite like this in our samples, but that flare seems to have finished our work for us. Until then, we had everything under control, and I was keeping our actual success hidden."

"So you didn't want to kill the Martians, but you did starve the survivors on the station?"

Sascha took a long breath. "What else were we to do? I know it wasn't the right thing, and I was slowly working on how to eliminate all the research and everyone involved, which was all of us. We can't let these corpos and the Union get a legal bioweapon. I could only remotely lock the computers in the science lab from the command station but couldn't wipe them. And then..." He trailed off. "I don't have a right answer. We messed up. I tried my best to keep this from getting it out, but now everything is being delivered to the Union on a silver platter."

Logan turned off the comms while scratching the back of his head. The air scrubbers whined at a higher pitch with the additional nine survivors. Logan got out of his seat and floated down the hallway toward the lab, careful to not bump his splinted arm. It itched under the splint. But it was more than that, like a feather tickled his entire body.

Liu looked up from her workstation as Logan entered. "Hey, how's the arm?"

"It's fine. How are you?"

"Still a little shaken that I couldn't save Carlos. I'm sorry."

"It's not your fault. You did your best. This was only supposed to be a recovery mission. Hell, we were only *supposed* to build an outpost well away from any real danger. . ."

She looked down for a few seconds at the microscope. "Logan, how are you feeling? Other than the arm I mean."

Still holding onto the entry port of the lab with his one free hand, Logan looked down the narrow hallway. "I miss my family."

"I can imagine. I can't wait to get back home, myself. Maybe finally retire after all this hazard pay." She chuckled.

He looked at Liu's microscope and her scratching her arm. After a long pause, he spoke in a low tone. "It got past the barrier, didn't it?"

She sighed. "It seems so, and I'm not sure what to do."

He wanted to scratch his whole body. Like cysts under his skin, solid lumps formed in his body, growing outward. "We need to talk. With the whole crew. Meet me in the mess hall in five. I'll fetch everyone else."

With everyone holding onto bars in the mess, Logan told them about what Sasha had been trying to do. Trying to prevent the Union from simply eradicating all the Martians, presumably to start over with fresh colonists. And now they were on the way back with all the data and live samples to boot. And the infection was on this side of the barrier too.

Jennifer clenched her bar till her knuckles were white. "Unacceptable! I have family on Mars!"

Logan turned to her. "Yes, but you have to understand the position I am in. You all know about my wife's condition. If I do anything out of line, then my wife will live a life of agony. I can't have that either. And of course, everyone's pay would be docked if we rebelled. Maybe even be turned over to the authorities."

A protracted silence took over the room.

"What if..." Logan started over. "What is the most moral thing to do here?"

"Not turn over the research, even if it means helping the Martians," Andrew offered. "Everyone knows my opinion of the rebellion, but infecting them is still messed up."

Liu shook her head. "But how do we do that?"

Andrew shrugged. "What if we warned the rebels?"

"Isn't all communication from our ship monitored?"

Jennifer spoke up. "What if we self-destructed the ship?"

Liu arched her eyebrows. "What? You passed the psyche evaluations!"

Jennifer shrugged. "I'm not crazy. But we need to prevent this from infecting everyone on Mars. And my brother."

Logan shook his head. "We couldn't even self-destruct because of the code it sends out, and then those of us with families wouldn't get any continued health insurance." Logan looked intently at everyone before settling on Jennifer. "Don't you have experience on the shuttle comm system? Do you think you could reconfigure the shuttle so the communication can't be monitored? You could send a targeted message to your brother to warn them."

Andrew cocked his head. "And what good would that do?"

Logan rubbed his head. "The rebellion does have ships. But they usually stay away from Mars, so they don't get destroyed by the Union warships. Maybe they could intercept us? But it would be risky to bring us on board. Unless they just made 'the problem' disappear..."

They discussed their options for a few minutes and came to an agreement.

The next few weeks of traveling were tense, and nobody liked that they could not send any messages to their friends or family. Logan locked down all communications.

They were getting uncomfortably close to Earth now. Only a few more days, and they would be in Earth orbit, where a Union warship waited for them.

Logan and the others decided to tell the survivors from the station nothing. Another questionable decision, but they didn't want anyone trying to stop them, even if they all likely agreed. And they continued isolating the survivors in the cargo hold. It did not matter much anyway, as half of them had died. The growths had grown to several feet long on those from the station, and it seemed there was a point when their bodies could not take it anymore.

Logan sat on the bridge looking at the radar and monitors. He struggled to sit back. A growth coming out of his back pushed him forward in the seat. A display showing two unfamiliar objects coming from their starboard side caught his attention. He called up the crew over the intercom.

Logan pointed at the monitor. "It appears that a couple of Union strike cruisers are heading our way. I've already contacted MC, and Union HQ has assured us they're not with the Union. Their closest warship is now enroute, but these strike cruisers will get to us first."

"Looks like some ships did defect," Carlos slapped Andrew's back, shaking the protrusions on both of them. "That's fifty bucks, buddy."

Andrew groaned.

Liu looked out at the stars. "So I guess this is my retirement, huh?"

Logan pulled out the bottle of Scotch he had brought from his quarters. He uncorked it. "I guess this is it. It's been an honor to work with you all." He hoped his wife would get a nice settlement and continued infusions.

A warning chime went off, indicating the computer had identified open weapon ports on a nearby ship.

"For Thomas," Logan said before taking a swig. He passed the bottle to Jennifer.

Yellow lights flashed on the bridge. They were being actively targeted.

She took a swig. "For doing the right thing." She passed it to Andrew.

An open radio broadcast came from the speakers. "Viva la rebellion!"

Andrew sighed and took a swig. "For peace." He passed it to Liu.

Sirens went off and the lights now flashed red. The ship's computer had identified a missile heading toward them.

Liu chuckled. "For my retirement! So short, but with good company." She took a few swigs before passing it to Carlos.

"For your wife, Nina," Carlos said and made a mock raising of the bottle to Logan.

Logan looked out the window. His vision blurred, and he barely made out what looked like a tiny comet that slowly revealed itself and flew to the *ISR Nebula.*

THE FLAMINGO CANTINA WARLOCK

Matthew Knight

Backstreet Drug Lord Bust! Detective Team does it Again! The headlines jumped out at me like dollar signs in neon lights when I opened the newspaper Monday morning. I was pleased to see a nice article done up about the latest crime case my partner, Rockwell, and I just put to rest. A gang of scumbags were running a drug ring downtown. We jumped them in a surprise attack Saturday night behind the Black Cat, beat em' down and took the leader by force. The kingpin fell at the mercy of my Colt .38 Special, and is now rotting behind bars, giving Rockwell and I the reputation as the two finest private eyes in the league.

I was in the office taking calls and reading those bold headlines over and over when the old, wooden grandfather clock down the hall groaned. I set down the paper and looked at my pocket watch to see that it was getting close to lunch. With no jobs on the books for the day, I planned to spend the afternoon at my favorite cocktail lounge, blowing some of the hard-earned cash I'd reaped from this latest success. Rising from my desk, I put on my raincoat and went to grab my hat when I heard a knock at the door.

"Come in," I said, expecting it to be Rockwell, trying to bum a ride to the lounge as usual.

When the door opened, I was surprised to find a young brunette standing in the entrance instead. Dressed in black furs and a long, form-fitting skirt, her shadowy eyes regarded me beneath a brimmed, laced hat. My attention was drawn to her dark red lipstick, as deep a shade as bulls' blood.

"Detective Wilcox?" the woman spoke in a breathy voice that suggested an air of softness and sensuality.

"Yes," I smiled, "What can I do for you ma'am?"

"I was wondering if I might have a moment of your time. I may have a case for you."

"Why, certainly," I said, removing my coat and returning it to the rack, "Won't you come in?"

"Thank you." The young lady entered my office. I quietly pulled the door closed behind her.

"May I take your coat?" I asked.

"I won't be long," she replied.

"Please have a seat," I pulled out the chair across from my desk.

Once she was seated, I got into position behind my desk, pulled the antique cigarette case from my pocket and opened it.

"Smoke?" I asked, offering her a cigarette.

"Don't mind if I do," she said, pulling a freshly rolled length from the case and putting it to her crimson lips.

I smiled and flicked the flint of my favorite lighter made of polished silver. She leaned forward seductively as I lit the cigarette for her. With a long inhale, she sat back, her dark eyes gleaming in the light of my desk lamp.

"And what can I do for you Ms..."

"Collins," she said, "Laura Collins."

"Ms. Collins," I acknowledged while lighting up a smoke for myself.

"Well, you see, detective."

"Please," I interrupted, lounging back, "Call me Harvey."

"Harvey..." she continued, "My cousin Helen and I are in town from upstate. We had originally only intended to be here for a short while to attend a lecture, but decided to stay a bit longer and make the trip a bit of a vacation. We're lodging at the Flamingo Cantina resort downtown."

"That's a fancy joint," I said, "Only rich folks stay there."

"Yes, well... the reason I'm here, Harvey, is that Helen has gone missing. She went out two days ago and has not returned or tried to contact me since. We are very close and I find this highly unlike her."

"Have you inquired with the police?"

"Yes, of course. They say that they're doing all they can. But there's more..." Her eyes shifted nervously. A shadow darkened her countenance as she leaned away from warm glow of the lamp.

"The penthouse upstairs is occupied by a suspicious-looking man who stays up all hours of the night. I've noticed strange things going on there lately."

"What kinds of things?" I asked.

"Chanting, weird howls in the middle of the night, women in robes coming and going, occasional lights and smoke of odd colors visible through the windows. It frightens me!"

"And the resort staff are aware of this?"

"Yes, they don't seem to want to bother the man. They say to leave him alone as if he is too important to disturb. The police say he's harmless as well. I don't know, Harvey, but something tells me that Helen's disappearance is somehow connected to these queer happenings. Is there anything you can do?

"We'll need some solid evidence," I said, "I'll go up to the Cantina and have a look around. You've got me interested in this character, and I'd like to see some of these strange things for myself."

I stubbed out the cigarette in the ash tray and stood up, grabbing my coat and hat.

"Come on," I said, "I'll give you a ride into town. I want to check out this penthouse during the daylight hours. I'll get some answers for you, Ms. Collins, one way or another."

We left the office and hopped into my Plymouth Special Deluxe 2-door. With the sun visor down, I drove Ms. Collins into town, dropped her off at a hair parlor near the Flamingo Cantina, and headed to the resort to have a look around.

I parked the car and went inside. The Flamingo was the biggest resort in the city. It was high class; as fancy of a joint as you'd find around these parts. As tempted as I was to stop for a Rob Roy in one of their fine lounges, I reminded myself I was there on business.

I walked along the shiny, marble floor of the lobby. Strolling through crowds of people, passing plush couches and luxurious fountains, I eventually reached an elevator. I rode it up to the penthouse suite then followed a long red carpeted hall until I found a tall wooden door. I knocked loudly. No response. I added some extra force the second time and it opened.

A woman in a red, silken, night dress was poised behind the heavy door. The dress ended just above her knees and she was barefoot. She had long, wavy, black hair that looked a mess. Her dark brows narrowed when she saw me and her eyes looked hazy. I figured she was drugged.

"Can I help you?" she asked with a thick Italian accent.

"Good Afternoon, Miss," I said, tipping my hat, "I'm looking for the gentleman who rents this suite."

"He is not here." she replied in an agitated voice, eying me up and down.

"Oh, I see. Well, I'm Wilcox...Detective Wilcox. I'm on the case of a missing girl and was wondering if you folks might happen to..."

"No," she said.

I saw through the doorway that on the wall behind her was a large painting of some otherworldly creature that resembled a giant toad. Glancing down, I then noticed that on the woman's right hand was some sort of stain that looked like dried blood.

"Well, would you mind if I came in and had a look around? We're taking precautions, you see and..."

"When he returns." she interrupted again and slammed the door in my face.

"Wait, Miss!" I grabbed the knob and tried to turn it. It was locked. I banged on the door again. There was no response.

I turned around and high tailed away from the place. Ms. Collins was right. Something seemed fishy about this place, and I intended to get to the bottom of it.

That night I phoned up Rockwell to fill him in. We made plans to bust into the suite and scope things out.

I picked him up at the lounge just around 11:00 PM. It was pouring rain when the stocky detective jumped into the car and we headed out to the Cantina. He had with him a brown, burlap sack.

"You got the rope?" I asked.

"Yeah, yeah, I got it," he said, pulling from the sack a wound-up length of tightly woven, white sailors' rope with a large, metal grappling hook at the end, "What makes you think this guy won't just let us in anyway?"

"Trust me," I said, "I get the feeling from talking with that broad that they are hiding something in there. We need to creep up unaware."

"Whatever you say, Wilcox," Rockwell sighed, "Although, I must confess, I'm no fan of climbing in the rain."

"Leave that to me." I said, "You just meet me inside when I give the signal."

We arrived, parked on the far side of the lot behind a plastic palm tree, and cased the joint for a moment. There penthouse suite appeared dark.

"Our man must've gone out for the evening," said Rockwell.

"Let's hope so," I said opening the car door, "Stay here. When I give the signal that the coast is clear, you go inside up to the top floor, and I'll let you in."

"Right, boss," he said.

I walked casually in the shadows along the edge of the parking lot through the rain, carrying the wound up rope concealed beneath the left breast of my long coat. When I got near the far left corner of the lot, I made a dash across the blacktop to the building, all the way to the rear wall leading up to the penthouse. I gazed up through the rain at the high balcony above me.

I began swinging the end of the rope like a windmill, gathering momentum. Releasing it, I tossed the cord high up to the balcony railing. When it hit, I pulled the rope tought until I felt the grappling hook bite firmly into the ledge. After a test to assure myself it would support my weight, I started climbing. The rainfall made it difficult, causing my leather gloves to slip a bit, but I was a fast climber. Moving as a vertical shadow in the neon light of a cabana sign, after avoiding a few windows, I was at the top.

Pulling myself up and over the ledge, I found I was on a nicely furnished platform with plants and a little breakfast table set up. I ducked low and looked about. All was still and it appeared that no one had taken notice of me climbing up there. There were two swinging glass doors leading into the penthouse from the balcony. Peering through them, I saw that it was still dark inside. Rockwell was right. Apparently the man and his lady had gone out for the night. I tried the door handle and of course, it was locked.

Busting through the glass would've been easy enough, but might've caused alarm, so I took from my coat pocket a handy device I had created; a compass – like the kind you use in geometry class as a kid, only this one had a hard diamond point on the end, sharp as a shark's tooth. I'd acquired it when I was in the African mines two years prior. The thing was a cat burglar's dream.

With steady hands, I put the compass to the glass and started etching. Round n' round I turned it, slowly so the shrill, high-pitched noise it made wasn't heard. Eventually the point dug in deep enough so that I felt the circle I'd made loosen up. Carefully, I pulled free the glass disc, revealing a perfectly round hole near the door knob just big enough for my hand to fit into. Reaching in, I unlocked the door and turned the knob.

Quickly leaning over the balcony rail, I gave the signal to Rockwell who was still waiting in the car. Once he exited the vehicle and walked inside, I entered the penthouse.

By the light of a small flashlight, I crept from the balcony into the main living room area and scoped out the pad. It was decked out real nice. High class furniture, antique lamps, exotic potted plants, and vases of amberina glass adorned the main room. There was an expensive record player at hand and some 45s on the coffee table - Chopin, Rachmaninoff, Barlioz and some other deadbeat stuff, as well as Charlie Parker and Dizzy Gillespie, which was more up my alley, and probably what he threw on for the ladies. Also, on the coffee table was an ashtray loaded with cigarette butts, several of which had lipstick smeared on the ends – different colors too, which made me think this guy was a swift cookie with the dames.

There was a beautiful bar cart filled with decanters of fine liquors, and I must confess that once again I had to restrain myself from indulging in a drink. As I admired the booze selection, I found a long, ivory pipe; with a black residue of opium inside – the same stuff that drug gang we had just busted was selling. This sealed the deal; even if it turned out there was no funny business going on related to the girl, I could still rat him out to the cops for some cash on the side.

As I continued inspecting the place, I came across an odd spectacle; set up against the center wall of the living room was a shrine or altar of some sort. Upon an onyx pillar sat the two-foot tall statue of a weird creature, carved out of stone. The figure was squat, pot-bellied and had the likeness of a giant toad. It had sleepy eyelids that hung over globular eyes. It's large, grinning mouth revealed sharp teeth and its upturned snout was like that of a bat. . I remembered it as the same grotesque thing I saw depicted in the painting through the doorway when I chatted with the Italian broad earlier.

In front of the pillar was a red pillow on a small rectangular stool apparently for kneeling. Next to it was a stack of old-looking, leather-bound books with occult symbols burned into the covers.

As I shined the light upon the wall, I saw more framed paintings of exquisite quality, all depicting this same hideous being in various scenarios. The artwork was top notch and the setting for each appeared to be in some fantastic world. This guy was obviously infatuated with the creature.

There was a light tapping at the door. I went over to it and looked through the peep-hole. It was Rockwell.

"What took you so long?" I asked as I let him in.

"Some cocktail waitress was trying to spark something up with me. Find anything?"

"Yeah - a pipe with opium residue along with some weird statue and occult books. This cat's definitely bad news. If nothing else, he might be somehow connected to last week's drug bust. The residue is from the same stuff those thugs had."

Suddenly, there was a muffled cry coming from the bedroom. We rushed in and I hit the light switch. Upon the bed was a young lady — gagged and bound to the bed posts by her wrists and ankles. She was fair and blonde, dressed in a white, silken night dress. She had a busted lip and tears streamed down her face as she urgently tried to speak.

"Helen!" I ran over to the bed.

Rockwell and I quickly cut her bonds and removed the gag. The distressed girl fell bawling into my arms.

"How did you know my name?" She sobbed.

"Easy, doll," I said, trying to comfort her, "I'm Harvey Wilcox and this is Bruno Rockwell. Your cousin hired us to find you. We're going to see to it that the rat who did this does hard time."

"Oh, thank you so much." she cried in my arms for a moment then suddenly sat up.

"But you must hurry!" she said, "Donald Murray is more than an eccentric criminal. He's a demented warlock. Right now he's down at the back alley behind Nikko's Emporium with Frederica. They have another girl named Geneviève held captive, and plan to sacrifice her at midnight. They say she'll be offered to some ancient god whom they will summon tonight!"

"What kind of nonsense are you talking, girl?" I said, "You mean the thing represented by that stone idol in the living room?"

"Yes. It's no fairy tale. Being stuck with these two for the last few days, I've seen and heard things you wouldn't believe. It's horrible!"

"Frederica is the Italian bird?" I asked.

"That's right. She's a witch in Murray's service. Whether you believe me or not, Geneviève's in grave danger. Tonight's the night and you must hurry!"

I tossed Rockwell my keys.

"Take Helen to the police station and meet me behind Nikko's Emporium. We're going to nail this clown."

The Emporium was just a few blocks from the Cantina. I was on foot, hustling along the sidewalk through the rain, hoping to get to the girl before this Murray fellow did anything drastic.

This was the rough end of town but being that it was a weeknight, aside from the usual night owls and street prowlers, most of the city folk seemed to be settled in for the evening. I whizzed past a few drunken beggars and a familiar street corner woman who tried to get my attention. I threw a nickel to a bum and nodded to the lady that I'd take a rain check.

Turning on the block that led to the back alley behind Nikko's, I stopped at the corner. I heard some loud talking coming from behind the building and saw some people back there. Hugging to the brick wall, I entered the wide alley unseen. I crept over to a spot where some trash cans were, crouched low behind them and drew my Colt .38 Special. From here I could get a load of the wild scenario.

The man I figured to be Murray stood before an empty space in the alley reading from an old book. Helen was insistent on how dangerous the guy was. To me, he looked like he belonged in the circus; tall and slender with shoulder-length brown hair, a black, handlebar mustache curled above his thin lips. He had a ski-slope nose and a waxed, cone-shaped beard that jutted from his chin. The so-called warlock wore a yellow robe with bright green symbols upon it as well as a flowing, purple and black cape. He had created a circle of black, burning candles on the ground in the empty space that was near a chain-link fence. This he faced with glaring, bloodshot eyes, raving like a lunatic.

In the center of the circle was the young lass described by Helen as Geneviève; a petite redhead in a torn ceremonial gown. Gagged and bound at her wrists and ankles by hemp rope, she wept helplessly on the filthy ground.

Standing by was the dark-haired lady, Frederica, dressed in a scarlet tunic with tight black velvet pants and once again looking high as a kite. Armed with a .45 caliber Auto Ordinance sub machine gun, as well as a Colt 1911 semi-automatic sidearm of the same caliber, this gal was locked and loaded. Her eyes darted around nervously while she stood watch.

The madman chanted as I thought to myself how crazy these thugs were to have staged this charade in public.

"*Oh, great god of Hyperborea, the one called Tsathoggua, and Zhothaqquah, who reigns over the planet, Cykranosh and holds the Door to Saturn... Grace us with your presence this night!*"

"Freeze!" I stood up and aimed my pistol at Frederica. "Put down your weapons and release the girl."

The surprised warlock turned toward me and sneered.

"Take care of him, Frederica. Let no one interfere!"

Before I could react, that witch threw a small round object at the ground between us. It shattered and instantly a cloud of thick, sulphurous, red vapor filled the air, completely blinding me. I shot at her through the dense stuff and missed, as at that same moment, a hail of bullets was fired at me from Frederica's machine gun. I leaped and tumbled across the ground, dodging the shots, so that only the row of trash cans took the lead.

Dodging another clumsy spray from the witch's gun, I fired another shot. It hit Frederica in the side and she went down.

I put the warlock dead in my sights.

"Give it up, Murray," I said, "Your days of drug laundering, kidnapping, and devil worship are over!"

The warlock ignored me and continued reciting from the book. I dashed over to seize the girl, and get her out of harm's way before taking him down. Murray paused as he saw me approaching. Using a Mumyou-Ryu technique, he threw a long pointed dagger which cut through the fabric of my coat arm, just grazing my flesh. He then quickly spat out more gibberish.

"*Tsathoggua, who drinks the blood of the Elk Goddess, Youndeh, come forth from your throne! In the name of the great sorcerer, Eibon, Morghi, and Santampra Zeiros... Iqhui dlosh odhqlonqh... Hziulquoigmnzhah!*"

After he read these last few lines, the ground began to tremble as if the earth was quaking. The surprise knocked me off my feet. Great winds blew through the corridor created by the alleyway as lightning flashed in the sky. The ground shifted and a large crack began to form in the blacktop beneath

Geneviève. The poor girl was still inside the circle of candles, which amazingly remained burning despite the strong winds.

"Yes! Come forth, great lord!"

The sorcerer fell to his knees and spread his arms, looking up at the sky.

As the madman reveled in his triumph, I crawled towards Geneviève. Nearing the circle, I reeled back as something incredible happened. The crack crumbled and expanded into a great fissure so that a huge chasm gaped in the street where the circle had been. The girl was swallowed by its blackness.

To my horror and astonishment, a multitude of long, green tentacles rose from the pit. Several held Geneviève in their grasp while the others writhed in the air like alien tendrils. The girl screamed in terror as the snaky appendages caressed her.

I gazed wide-eyed as Murray laughed hysterically.

Then a great figure materialized in the circle, towering high over the mass of flailing tentacles. It was the creature I saw depicted by the statue at the warlock's penthouse. Furry and stout, it stood like a mutant toad on enormous haunches with its arms folded. As tall as a suburban house, it had large pointed ears like that of some prehistoric rodent. Black, bulbous eyes stared down at us and it grinned, displaying glistening fangs beneath its bat-like snout. The creature's being was of a spectral green substance, and was translucent. It stood silent and motionless, leering down at the naïve lunatic who called it forth.

Murray was ecstatic.

"Tsathoggua! Oh, Great One, how I have yearned for this day! Please accept this sacrifice and grant me the dark knowledge I seek! I have worshipped and paid tribute to you in many ways, for I have done as the book says."

The creature looked down at Geneviève who was trapped helplessly in the coils of the writhing tentacles, then addressed the warlock, speaking in a deep and thunderous voice that sounded as if it was echoing through a great cavern.

"I have no use for that which you offer, mortal." it said, "You of Earth and Sea and Sky have long since failed in you attempts to please the Elder Gods."

The tentacles holding Geneviève relaxed and laid her onto the ground. I quickly rushed over, warily scooped her up in my arms, and moved her away from the phantasmagoric pit. She was covered in a queer slime that smelled of oily reptiles. Murray no longer took notice of us, as the monstrosity continued.

"The Book of Eibon was written in the ancient Cykranoshian language that is not for your kind to know. Now that you have somehow inherited the forbidden knowledge, you must be removed from this world and imprisoned in the ultra-mundane deeps, so that no other earthly beings should surmise that which you have learned. In the dark Hells beneath Mount Voormithadreth you will serve us for eternity."

Murray trembled on his knees, mouth agape. Tears streamed down his face and he began laughing hysterically. Suddenly, the tentacles reached out and violently seized him. The warlock screamed in terror, as they coiled around his limbs, lifting him into the air. The flailing mass then withdrew itself and vanished into the chasm, pulling Murray down with it.

The creature called Tsathoggua turned its bulging eyes down toward me and Geneviève.

"Thin is the veil betwixt Earth and the Old Ones' primordial realms." it said, "Heed my words and meddle not in the affairs of the gods, or all of mankind may suffer a fate similar to that of this fool. Let my words be a warning to you and all of your kind."

"Wilcox!"

I turned around to see Rockwell and half a dozen police officers carrying pump shotguns come running into the alley.

"Get back!" one of them shouted before they all opened fire at the giant monster. With the girl in my arms I dashed out of the way and leaned up against the side of the building while shots blasted. I knew what they were doing was useless. The bullets went right through the spectral image of the ancient deity.

Thsathoggua glanced at me once more and grinned slyly. His image then faded into thin air so that all that was left was a great hole in the blacktop.

Rockwell ran over to help me cut Genevieve's bonds.

"Heavens, man, what was that thing? Some illusionary trick that magician pulled off?"

"I imagine so." I said entranced.

"Are you alright, Harvey? You look like you've seen a ghost."

"Yeah," I answered, ungagging the girl, "Just a little shook up from that earthquake."

More cops showed up and were now swarming like ants, surveying the scene. I looked over to see one of them handcuffing Frederica, who had now come to. Somehow she survived the shot she took. The witch spat and shot me an evil eye as they shoved her into the back of a paddy wagon.

"What of Donald Murray?" asked Rockwell, "Did he get away?"

"No," I pointed to the enormous hole.

"He fell down there?"

I nodded.

"Good work, Wilcox," a gruff voice said.

I turned to see Commissioner Sanford in his brown raincoat holding that wretched book the warlock used to summon the devil.

"Not only have you saved the kidnapped girls, but this priceless book was stolen from the city museum months ago. We've had another team of private eyes on the case of hunting it down, and once again it was you who came through. You can count on receiving a large check in the mail from the museum, as well as Laura Collins' secretary. Collins is a millionaire, you know."

"Thanks, commissioner," I said, still staring dazedly at the black fissure.

Sanford nodded and walked away, taking the young lady with him.

"Haha! Hear that, boss?" Rockwell said, slapping me on the back, "We're gonna be fat cats come next week! Let's go celebrate."

"Congratulations, Harvey," a familiar voice interrupted.

Looking up, I beheld a female figure wearing a mink shawl over a form-fitting, sparkly dress. With a leather gloved hand she raised a long stemmed cigarette to her crimson lips, smiling as she swayed closer. It was Laura Collins. Seeing the raven-haired beauty once again instantly brought me back to my senses.

"Why, thank you, ma'am," I said, tipping my hat, "I told you we'd find Helen one way or another."

"You've done much more than that," she said, "Rest assured, you will be handsomely rewarded."

Giving me her arm, she leaned in close. I inhaled her perfume, feeling the warmth of her sleek body next to mine. She gave me a seductive look with those dark eyes, hinting that she intended on giving me more than money as a reward. I smiled in satisfaction.

"Well, Ms. Collins," I said as we began strolling arm in arm, "We were just about to celebrate. Where do you wanna go for a Scotch on me?"

She looked me in the eye and said,

"Anywhere but the Flamingo Cantina."

THE GIFT OF MALANKOMAS

Rick M. Clausen

Will Crabb was exhausted. He had gone ten grueling rounds with Hector Pennington, and he was worn to the seed. He had to keep his energy level and stay the course, or go down to the sod in defeat. With an unlimited number of rounds in bare-knuckle boxing, whoever dropped first and stayed dropped, was trounced. If you hadn't come to scratch, then you were done. That's the way it is with the illegal but sanctioned, bare-knuckle Pugilistic Foundation.

Will was strapping and tenacious but he couldn't put the man down. He could slug it out with the best of them, but his head was being pummeled, and his body ached in places he never could have imagined. With legs feeling like straw, he was relieved that the Foundation had finally disqualified kicking.

The purse was important but it didn't matter as much as his pride. It was the camaraderie of the ring, that's what mattered. How he stacked up, his visceral courage, that always mattered.

But now he was under the harrow. Blood was oozing from the punishing cuts around his eyes, making him shake his head to clear his vision. He forgot the pain from the raw mess that dripped from his bare knuckles, he just wanted the man facing him to go down. Will knew he could settle this with one punch. One good uppercut, or even a haymaker would finish this donnybrook.

But besides his blood, he was leaking vigor and stamina, and Pennington was taking advantage of it. His opponent was a sizeable man, with a stocky physique and enormous arms. Will had the longer reach and was holding him at bay, but Pennington was quick with the jabs.

As the rounds advanced, they often went into chancery, but the audience would have none of that. The crowd craved a fight, not two men dancing in a clinch.

Battered and bruised, both fighters circled each other and finally came to drub, toe to toe. Will threw a feint, hoping he could cross punch, but his opponent landed an unseen hook, then suddenly - everything went black.

Cobwebs of consciousness appeared out of the din, and Will heard his name being called. He found himself laying on a cot, where the overhead ceiling of a tent came into focus. The bedraggled face of Obediah, his manager, drifted into view. The conquered pugilist reached for the cold towel that draped his forehead and asked, "What happened?"

"You were out for a spell," said Obediah. "Overcome by a left hook. I keep telling ya, protect yer head more."

Crabb rubbed his battered head, as it seemed every hair on it hurt, but the fuzzy stars were finally dissipating. Damn, he relented, I squandered that one. He knew he could scrap and hold the field, and had done so in the past, but lately his luck wasn't showing its hand, and in this game you can't make any money coming in second place. Losing his following, no one would bank on him, and if that continued, he wouldn't even get a match.

"Cheer up, my boy," offered a familiar voice.

A tall man's shadowy figure stood by the tent flap, blocking the glare of the afternoon light. As Crabb's eyes adjusted to his surroundings, he smiled when he recognized his friend, Professor Byron Tate.

"Clear your head and wrap those hands," said the man. "You'll do better next time."

Yeah, next time, thought Crabb. His best supporter, the Professor, was an odd friend but he was always in the audience to root him on.

The man has to move more and watch his head, thought the Professor. It's a simple procedure, but the fight game is never simple. A sixty-two year old partisan of bare-knuckle brawling, the Professor knew the confinements of a dueling combatant. In his youth, he loved the physical contact, and he often reminisced about his formidable time in that ringed arena.

Decades ago, Barnabas Hensley taught him a good lesson. If he wanted to reach the other side of his twenty-five years, he had to quit before the bell pealed at his twenty-sixth.

Will Crabb was his enlisted hero because the fighter wouldn't give up. His faith in the pugilist was the man's skill, his courage, and his strength in taking a punch well. The problem concerning the educated scholar lately, was the tendency of his boxer of taking too many punches. He was afraid his topmost fisticuffer would become a sodden palooka, a punching bag for the contenders.

A distinguished astronomer, the Professor's title of star-gazer would often alternate to his

role of star-maker. He would recommend to Obediah to give the man a rest. A few days at the beach would calm his apprehension, clear the fighter's head, and heal those roughshod hands.

Along the coast of Oregon, not far from Coos Bay, the university town of Norcrest was enjoying a fine spring day. The colder currents of the Pacific ocean had made their way north and that made the waters warm, the temperature mild, and allowing small cresting waves on the shoreline. Somewhat early for sunbathers, the seagulls could be heard squawking and scolding each other as they fought for the dregs along the shore of the small beach.

The salty sweat from Crabb's brow slid down and stung the abrasions on his face. He wiped his head with a towel and was careful of the bruise under his right eye as he readjusted his sunglasses. The afternoon sun felt good on his wounds, a faithful elixir wherever one lives. Straightening his beach chair, he gazed out over the Pacific. The briny air smelled good as he found himself mesmerized by the unceasing rhythm of the breakers.

"Would ya look at this," came the voice of his manager next to him. He was holding up a newspaper exposing the sports page. "It says here that the Chicago Bears football team walloped the Green Bay Packers last week."

"I'll bet Bronko Nagurski had a hand in that," answered Crabb with a smile.

"You're right," said Obediah sitting up straight. "It says he threw four passes in the game, besides being the leading rushing Fullback."

"Does it say anything about his wrestling bouts?" asked Crabb.

"Nah, he does that in the football off-season, you know that."

"I always wondered why he didn't strap and become a bare-knuckle boxer. He's certainly good at chancery."

"He probably doesn't want to get his pretty face messed up," offered Obediah. "Besides, he's making more money during these times than anybody I know."

Obediah laid back in his beach chair and closed his eyes. He remembered what it was like before the upheaval of the stock market crash. Before prohibition, and still illegal, he recalled how easy it was to find a scrap then. Any working class piker would stake a shot and wager on first blood alone. Even before bare-knuckle became sanctioned, the plungers would bear the palm and side bets would spring up like a sale on women's silk stockings.

Crabb stretched his legs and peered at the sky. His thoughts went to his last fracas. How did he lose that fight, he wondered? He never saw the hook coming, yet he prepared for it. He grappled with Pennington just minutes before, yet he was suckered into that punch. He ran his fingers through his hair as he remembered he had fallen for that trick before. Regrettably, he knew he had made too many mistakes.

"Whadda ya think Will?" pried Obediah, as he brushed the sand from his calves. He felt he was not the only one who was going to enjoy a rest from the ring. Managers had sore muscles too. Relaxing at Mather's beach was a good prescription from the professor. Besides, other pugilists and their managers found it soothing to unwind at the beach from time to time.

"I was thinking I shouldn't have lost that fight," said the gladiator, with rebellious scorn. He stood up and threw his sunglasses on the beach towel. "I'm going for a swim."

Crabb ran toward the ocean with his easy gait, then hit the surf with a splash before he dove further into the waves. He stroked and paddled his way, ignoring the numbing he could feel from the sea water on his sore and abraded wounds. He was making his way back to the beach when he felt his foot becoming tangled in something. Unable to touch the bottom, he continued to swim until he could touch the sand beneath him. Reaching down, he grabbed a slithery substance from around his leg and pulled it to the surface.

"Seaweed," he said out loud with disgust. Holding the glutinous algae outstretched in his hand, he trudged ashore with his find. As he waded onto the sand, he was about to drop it when he noticed something tangled in the brown twisted leaves of the kelp. It was dark and hard, unlike the soft and pliable plant itself. Dragging the thing over to where his manager was sitting, Obediah commented, "What ya got there?"

"I don't know exactly," Will replied. "Something's wrapped in this seaweed."

"Whew, it stinks," complained his manager. "Throw it away."

"No, there's something solid and twisted in here."

Crabb reached over to his beach bag and withdrew a pocketknife. He was hoping his find would reveal a nice seashell. The algae was tightly wound around the object and it took him several minutes to free the thingumabob from its glutinous confinement.

"What in the... ?" exclaimed the fighter.

The treasure from the sea was black as slate and rock-like hard. Slightly larger than a pack of cigarettes, it was almost square with smooth and rounded edges. Small markings were scratched around it, exposing a rough edge on one end.

Will grabbed his hand towel and rubbed around the object, cleaning it from the surf and sand. His hands ached, still sore from the fight, but he was excited to know what he had found.

"Whadda think of that!" he exclaimed, holding the object up in the air.

"Well, that's an interesting bit of shellfish ya have there," mocked Obediah.

"Yeah, isn't it?" replied Crabb. "Wonder where it came from?"

"Let me see it," gestured Obediah. He turned the object around in his hands, feeling the texture. "Doesn't look like coral, it's too smooth. And it's not very heavy for a rock."

"What do ya think it is?" questioned Crabb.

"Why don't ya ask your friend, the Professor. I'll bet he'd know."

Will had been to his friend's office only a couple of times before, and always felt inferior there. With no formal education, he thought colleges were complicated places. However, he always enjoyed the pictures of stars, planets, and solar systems that adorned the walls and kept company with the astronomer's library of books.

The door to the professor's office was just down the darkened hall in the scientific wing of the university building. When classes weren't in session, the college turned off most of the lights in the hallways to save electricity. It reminded Will of the ominous gray-bar hotel, a place where he infrequently spent the night after tossing down too many brew-skis.

He knocked on the office door and was greeted with a, "Come in."

The astrophysicist was seated at his desk and rose when Crabb entered.

"Will, my boy," said the man. "How are you doing and how are your hands holding up?"

"I'm fine, Byron, thanks," said the boxer. "Professor, I found an interesting thing on the beach the other day, and wonder if ya could help me with it."

Crabb placed the small cardboard box he was carrying on the Professor's desk.

The Professor opened the flaps and cautiously took out the object.

"Well, what do we have here?" he said.

The scientist studied long and hard at the rock-like figure as he turned it around in his hands. He then shook it and when it didn't rattle, he stated, "It certainly is light, isn't it?"

"Whadda ya think?" asked Crabb.

"I don't believe it's a meteorite," said the Professor, "It's so angular, so square. The sides are all flat, and the edges are all rounded. It has all the makings of being man-made.

"Why's it so light?" questioned Will.

"I'm not sure, but I think it may be a piece of pottery," said the man as he held it up to the overhead light. "You say you found it on the beach?"

"Yeah, wrapped in slimy seaweed."

"Seaweed, eh?" commented the Professor. "Was it kelp by any chance?"

"Yeah, I guess so. Brown, gummy leaves, and very stinky."

The Professor nodded his head in agreement. "Kelp has lasting properties. There are kelp forests all over the world. Some fronds use gas-filled floats that can carry the algae from ocean to ocean. I think you may have a pottery vessel that got caught in a kelp bed. Somehow, it became entangled and then transferred itself from one frond to another."

"What are those tiny scratches on it?" asked Will.

The Professor walked over to his desk drawer and retrieved a magnifying glass. He held the unusual little nomad close while he examined it thoroughly.

"They're very diminutive, but they look like etched animal or human figures," the Professor said.

"Ya said it's a vessel," posed Crabb. "Doesn't a vessel have an opening?"

"You would think so, huh? But it seems completely sealed," said the scientist. He brought the magnifying glass up again and said, "I may be wrong, but these could be ancient Greek letters marked here. The end of the piece is also odd. It's a blemish or deterioration as though a piece was missing, or maybe broke off."

"Whadda think?" queried Will.

"Well, archaeology is not my field, but I know someone who is, and I'll contact him and we'll go over this together. Why don't you come back tomorrow and we can discuss it then?"

"Sounds like a plan," replied Will.

When he left the professor's office that afternoon, Crabb felt he had found something curious and worthwhile. He didn't know what it was, but he wagered it may just be the good-luck token he was looking for.

After his friend left, the professor walked over to a small table next to an open window. He placed the artifact on the table, but he turned too quickly and his foot caught the leg of the table, jiggling it. The curio slipped off the edge and fell to the hardwood floor, breaking apart upon impact.

"Dammit!" exclaimed the man.

As he stooped to pick up the pieces, he found the artifact had only cracked in half. A separate part had now been exposed and was sticking out of the ceramic-ware, like a pea from its pod.

"Hello, what's this?" said the Professor in amazement, as he freed the tiny component.

Completely surrounded by a nest of straw, it was shaped like a crucible with an organic substance cradled in its basin. Curious about the pulp-like paste, he brought the piece up to his nose.

"Hmm," he murmured to himself, what an odd smell. But he wondered why the little terrine was sealed away? The Professor thought now would be a good time to contact his archaeologist colleague. The scientist again placed the artifact and its pieces very carefully on the table and then moved to his desk to make his telephone call.

The Northwestern Spring air was appreciably warm at this time of year and it allowed several of the college's windows to remain open in daylight. A gentle breeze wafted across the campus and whisked into the room of the professor, bringing with it a lone fly, soon followed by a meandering solitary black ant. The fly quickly found its way back out, but the ant crawled over to the little ceramic bin and waded into the ancient depository.

When the Professor returned to the table, he noticed the ant lumbering across the unfamiliar ingredients.

"Get out of there," he said, as he flicked the insect out of the tiny tray.

The ant rolled out and across the table but regained itself and began to scurry away. To rid himself of the nuisance, the Professor indifferently pressed his index finger on the insect to crush it. But the ant did not compress and continued its excursion. Perturbed, the man strategically placed his thumb over the invertebrate and pressed down. He removed his thumb, and the ant remained unmarred and unmangled. It was invincible to the pressure, for its legs, antenna, and all its segmented parts were undamaged. Baffled more than frustrated, the man slammed his fist down on the ant. But when he pulled his hand back, the diminutive critter just continued his course, unscathed.

"What kind of ointment did you step in?" the Professor said, with astonishment.

He quickly grabbed the glass ash tray from his desk and placed it on the table upside down over the ant to contain it. Fascinated, the man of science wondered what his colleague would say when he saw the might of his tiny new adversary.

The rain was falling steadily when Obediah and Crabb made their way to the office of the Professor. Spring in this part of the country can also be wet during this season, and Crabb felt lucky that he was able to get some sun on his tired body when he found his little treasure.

When the two men entered the Professor's office, they found the scientist standing by a window intently focused on something on the nearby table. He didn't acknowledge their entrance as Will greeted the man with, "Afternoon, Professor."

"Yes, yes, good afternoon," replied the Professor, without looking up.

He then nonchalantly walked over to his desk and sat down with a guarded sigh. He stared at a picture on the wall depicting an astronomical galaxy in all its star-stuff. Squinting his eyes, his inner mind formed the Periodic Table of chemical elements. He then leaned back with closed eyes, as molecular formulas danced in his head. The room was unusually subdued, with only the sonance of the ticking wall clock and the pitter-patter of the outside rain.

After a few quiet moments, Crabb offered, "Professor?"

The astrophysicist broke from his stupor and looked up at the pugilist. Tugging on his earlobe, a habit he had developed whenever he was perplexed, the Professor cleared his throat.

"Do you know what inertia is?" he asked, his tone was more hypothetical.

Puzzled, the two laymen looked at each other.

"You have a fascinating conundrum here," the Professor said, straightening himself in the chair. "I guess it's stranger than anything else." He shook his head and continued, "The markings on your little ceramic vessel are very ancient. They're Greek or maybe Cretan. They date back further than the Macedonians or even the Phoenicians."

"I don't know much about history, Professor," said Crabb, shyly.

"Yes, of course," said the Professor. "I did contact that colleague of mine, and we determined that this small artifact is around three thousand years old."

Amazed, the two journeymen glanced at each other again.

"My colleague believes this little find is Minoan in craftsmanship. It was kiln-fired, leaving it in a stone-like state. Like stone, it will not decompose readily, but it will break. I believe that's why it has survived this long." The Professor paused, and then said, "It probably fell overboard from an ancient ship or even a shipwreck, and then somehow got caught in some kelp bed."

The Professor rose from his chair and moved to the center of the room. He was used to lecturing and felt better on his feet.

"Those markings on that curio are certainly etched, but at some point may have actually been painted as well. The name of Achilles is there, along with several others."

"Achilles?" uttered Obediah. Not a learned man, but the veteran boxing trainer did know the hero of the Trojan War.

"Yes, the warrior was never defeated in battle," answered the Professor. "Hercules and Theseus are also represented, but one name stands out to me. An ancient Greek boxer known as,

Melankomas of Caria. He is the most recent of all the names listed."

"Why's he so special?" inquired Crabb. He had a genuine interest in these men of

antiquity, but was impatient with the history lesson.

"Melankomas was an Olympic boxing champion, a bare-knuckle fighter. They didn't use boxing gloves back in those days, you know," pontificated the Professor. "Living around 50 B.C., he went down in history as one of the most proficient fighters in the ancient world. There are some fables that say he could defeat his opponents without ever dealing a blow."

"Never a blow?" blurted Obediah, surprised.

"Such are the Greek fables," the Professor said, shrugging his shoulders. "The most captivating and certainly the most intriguing find, is the paste I found within the vessel."

"What paste?" said Crabb, his curiosity piqued.

"I'm sorry, Will," the Professor apologized. "I broke your artifact yesterday by accident. It fell off the table there and broke into two pieces. Bizarre as it was, it had another segment inside."

The Professor walked over to the table and picked up the little crucible. The two men gathered around him, anxious to see what he had.

"This little dish-like segment was found within the artifact, with this pasty organic substance on the bottom. I left it for a moment to make a call and when I returned, an ant had crawled into the paste and then exhibited some extraordinary assets," revealed the Professor. "It became impervious to any harm. That traipsing little six-legged Tarzan was indestructible!"

"Where's the ant now?" asked Crabb.

"My colleague, Professor Dutton in archaeology, has it. He's conducting some experiments on our petite friend."

"What kinda paste would do that?" questioned Obediah.

"The paste I believe, is really a balm or ointment for a warrior or athlete," answered the Professor. "The ancients would smear the salve over themselves before a battle or contest.

It was a ritual for all athletic combatants, but this particular elixir seems to have different properties."

"Like an armored cover?" inquired Crabb. He was aroused by the Professor's remark of, *indestructible.* His senses now became alert.

"What that substance is, gentlemen," the Professor said, in his lecturer mode, "is a non-submissive entity of nature. You could call it the perfect energy absorber. It seems to have the inertia of an untold amount of mass. Personally, I just don't understand how this could be."

Enticed, Crabb let the Professor's words fall without comprehension. If that salve could help him withstand a punch, he could be on easy street. He could be invincible!

"God almighty," exclaimed Crabb, "If I had that stuff on me ...!"

"I know some majordomos ..." began Obediah, with infectious excitement.

"Gentlemen, gentlemen," interrupted the Professor, his voice rising. "We are talking about wanton energy here. I'm trying to understand, to...to construe how all this energy converts to mass."

"Professor, does it make any difference?" said Crabb, half-heartedly.

"No, of course it doesn't," chimed in Obediah. Like his fighter, he didn't care about all the scientific mumble-jumble. If the salve would help him win fights, that's all that matters.

"I drew a small sample for testing," surrendered the Professor. "I'm having it analyzed as we speak."

"Well, let us know what ya come up with," replied Crabb as he grabbed the crucible. "In the meantime, we have to get ready to scratch!"

The day of Crabb's match was crisp, clean, and had all the smell-fresh ingredients that a day-after rain leaves behind. The gathered crowd was forming in small bunches, as crowds often do before a full-scale contest. The numerical legal tenders were exchanging hands as the eager gamblers plied their trade. The sod floor of the prepared hand-to-hand encounter was carefully raked and leveled, all the ropes around the circular ring were secured, and beer sales were up.

Crabb and Obediah walked with confidence to the ring, closely followed by their corner-man, Harvey Tucker. As soon as Crabb sat down on his stool, Obediah reached in their kit bag and brought out a carefully packaged container. Dipping his finger into the small receptacle, the manager began to smear the contents on Crabb's fists and forehead.

Crabb's opponent, Haroon Watson, soon appeared with his trainers and entered the ring. Watson was a huge, barrel-chested hunk with large hands, big ears, and a relatively undersized head. A strapping man, the weapon of choice was his stone-hard powerful punch.

The crowd began to murmur as everyone waited for the starting bell. As the first round began, there were many jabs and feints between the two men. Several hooks were thrown from Watson, but the punches seemed light and landed without force. They appeared to glace off Crabb as natural as rain on glass.

Wavering, Watson's pride was now ruffled and he stepped back from his opponent. He drew in a long breath, and then lunged forward. His left hand came up for a feint as his right hand cocked for a roundhouse. The bruiser then pulled the trigger and with all his might, the haymaker went for Crabb's head. Will didn't dodge, and the blow landed squarely against his jaw. As if poked with a pillow, Crabb's head barely moved, allowing only a flinch.

His opponent, however, had a different aftermath. Watson's level of force was immediate and forthright. The exerted punch was equal in power of bashing one's raw knuckles into an anvil. With a wail, the fighter dropped to his knees and grabbed what remained of his right hand. Crushed immediately, his metacarpals were pulverized in a pulp of blood and bone, suspended only by the laxity of flesh.

The round and the skirmish were deemed over in just under three minutes. There were cheers and jeers all around as Harvey patted Will's head with a towel and Obediah continued his backslapping.

In the weeks that followed, there developed a secession of fights for Crabb, all of which he easily won. He began to ascend the ladder of success and quickly arrived at the position of the leading sanctioned contender.

The Professor was pleased with Crabb's wins, but was concerned about the other opposing camps. He had heard from one trainer, that his own up-coming battler, Taw Sheppard, was unstoppable. Eager to observe this newcomer, the Professor made a notation to witness his next fight.

Sheppard, a large, bruising powerhouse, with thickset arms and legs, and a substantial punch, had reached the top levels in the bare-knuckle tintamarre.

There was to be one more semi-final engagement before the championship bout, and that would be with the formidable and unmatched Sean McMasters.

A massive, mountain of a man, McMasters was 6 feet 6 inches, with hands as large as cantaloupes and arms bigger than they had a right to be. An exceptionally strong individual, the

brute force of his steely blows could leave a knuckled tattoo in his opponent's head. McMasters was the top contender and appeared to be unbeatable. Through tight negotiations, he agreed to fight the much shorter Sheppard in the semi-final match.

Beneath the Eucalyptus and Red Alders of Esterpine, a village many miles from the college town of Norcrest, the roped circular ring of the sanctioned semi-final brouhaha awaited the fisticuffers. A day of clouds, the wind was favorable and the odds were square for the bookies and speculators. Teeming with tinhorns and bagmen, the throngs of wagerers crammed the area with their medley of beer and rye whiskey.

The Professor sat in the make-shift stands and watched intensely as Sheppard's manager and his corner-man prepared the eager pugilist. From a small box, Taw's handler dipped into a greasy substance and smeared the salve over the fighter's face and clenched hands.

The round began with the usual feints and jabs then minor strapping. At one point, McMasters tried to square up and joust Sheppard with his huge arms, but his opponent would have none of that and went into chancery. After a few seconds, the shorter man then pushed the taller man away. When McMasters dropped his guard, Sheppard quickly took one step forward and lashed out at the larger man with a braced, powerful right-hand uppercut to the jaw.

The reaction to the blow was immediate. McMasters' head snapped back as several teeth flew from his mouth. His legs quivered under him as his body straightened like a flagpole. Teetering, he tumbled backward and collapsed, much the same as a felled redwood tree. Unconscious before he hit the sod and with a shattered jaw, it was impossible for the combatant to come to scratch. The fray was over in two minutes and eight seconds.

Two days before the championship bout, Crabb and Obediah came to see the Professor. The boxer felt good about his prospects. He hadn't lost a fight since Watson, and his spirits were high. Obediah could sense the confidence in his fighter and knew they were on their way to the Bare-Knuckle Title.

When they entered the Professor's office, they noticed that the man seemed to be in one of his pensive moods again as he sat behind his desk studying Will's broken artifact. The more he turned and fingered the little curio, the more the lines of consternation formed on his face.

"You are about to make some serious wampum with this up-coming bout," said Crabb eagerly to his devoted friend. "I haven't lost a fight yet."

"Yes, it seems to be going that way," replied the Professor. He placed the artifact on the desk and turned his attention to his alter ego. "I understand you're going to fight Taw Sheppard."

"Yeah, a tough guy," said Crabb. "But he'll go down jus' like the rest."

"You know he beat Sean McMasters?" said the Professor, cautiously. He didn't want to patronize, but his concern was growing.

"So what? McMasters was big alright, but he was clumsy as an ox."

"Will?" said the Professor, the tone of empathy was in his voice. His manner of speaking now became deliberate. "Don't underestimate that man," he pleaded.

"Why? I have the salve. Nobody's gonna beat me."

"Yes, that emollient is extraordinary," the Professor agreed.

The scientist knew it seemed to have a touch of magic in its alchemy. The why and wherefore were the missing elements. The analysis came back with mostly familiar contents. Traces of menthol, olive oil, balsam, arnica and strychnine, and there were even analgesic herbs from the cinchona bark. All ingredients that were available in those ancient times, but there was nothing to prove the salve led to any sorcery or fiendishness, so what made it so dynamic?

Toying with the prospect of metaphysical or supernatural phenomena, he wondered what else might be instilled within those mystical properties?

The Sheppard-McMasters fight came to mind and the Professor considered telling the men about his unsolicited visitor a few weeks ago.

"Did you know Dewey Bolton came to see me the other day?" said the Professor calmly.

"No," answered Will, "Who's this Bolton?"

"He's Taw Sheppard's manager," he replied, delicately.

Crabb and Obediah exchanged glances. A frown appeared on the manager's face as he rubbed his nose. This doesn't sound good, he thought.

Crabb sucked in a gulp of air and placed his hands on his hips.

"What the hell's going on?" he said, indignantly. "Are ya switching sides now? I thought ya was my friend?"

"I am your friend, Will," said the Professor. "He came to me, I didn't go to him."

"Yeah, and everybody knows how irresistible ya are with bare-knuckle boxing," said Crabb, seething with anger. Sure, he thought, now that I'm at the top of the heap, people are looking for answers. If the Professor helped me, maybe he'll help them.

"Did he offer ya a piece of the pie?" persisted the pugilist. "Doesn't he know his fighter is gonna get his clock cleaned?"

"Will, it wasn't like that at all," cautioned the Professor.

"Jus' so we understand each other," stated Crabb, "*I* made it here. I'm the one who took

the hammering." He stood up straight, emphasizing his full height, and held out his clenched fists. "I don't know about that Greek glop, but I humped the blows with smashed hands and I'm the one who'll end up on top with all the simoleons!"

"We know that, Will," reassured Obediah.

"Of course, my boy," the Professor lamented.

"Jus' remember that," declared Crabb. He ran the fingers of one hand through his hair and rubbed the back of his neck. "It's stuffy in here. I need ta knock back a couple." He pointed his thumb at Obediah and said, "Ya wanna wet yer beak?"

"No," said his manager, "I've got some things to do. I'll see ya later, Will."

Hastily, Crabb headed for the door and the Professor blurted out, "Aren't you curious what Bolton wanted to see me about?"

"I don't give a damn what he wanted! I jus' hope your dedication deals with being in my corner when the bout starts."

With that, Crabb would hear no more and was out the door.

The Professor sat in his chair for a moment, staring at the artifact on his desk. He then got up, and with a large sigh, began to slowly pace the room. Shaking his head back and forth, he was clearly troubled.

"What exactly did Bolton want?" asked a concerned Obediah.

"I'm afraid we may have a problem," said the Professor, searching for the right words. His hands were behind his back and his head was bent as he continued, "While he and Sheppard were sunbathing on Mather's beach a few weeks ago, they found something odd and brought it to me for identification."

"And what was it?"

"It was an artifact much like what Will found," answered the scientist, pointing to the object on his desk.

"An artifact?"

"Yes, I'm afraid it rivaled your curio. It had little markings on the surface and was even rolled up in a ball of kelp, just like yours was."

The Professor then straightened up and turned to face Obediah.

"The most appealing thing is, the artifact had an end piece that was missing, just like Crabb's."

"Well, that *is* odd," said the manager. "Do ya think it's a coincidence?"

"That's not the half of it," the Professor said, dryly. "Instead of accidently dropping it, like I did, Bolton just cracked it open in front of me!"

"Jeez, what a great archaeologist he would make!" said his listener, sarcastically.

"There it was, a little crucible inside, again, just like Will's," said the Professor, reflecting his astonishment.

"So what's all this mean?" drawled Obediah.

"Apparently, Will's piece and Bolton's piece were attached together. They broke off somewhere in time."

"Somewhere in time?"

The Professor shook his head.

"I believe both artifacts were originally combined together, as one module. Somehow,

throughout the ages, they were separated, detached. Maybe a shipwreck or an earthquake, I don't know."

The Professor sauntered back over to his desk and sat down. He picked up Crabb's curio again and stared at it.

"Ya haven't mentioned the problem," declared Obediah.

The Professor turned to the man and said, "Look, Bolton later told me they had an incident with a fly, or I guess it was a mosquito." He paused for a moment, not quite sure he was believing what he was about to say.

"Anyway, this mosquito came into contact with the paste of their curio, just like our ant did. Only instead of being invincible as well as passive, it became aggressive. They tried to swat the damned thing, but it only continued to attack with ferocity. It didn't draw blood, it was just a steady series of spiral plunging and spinning. Bolton said its buzzing, reminded him of an aerial dive-bomber! They finally contained it with a frying pan!"

"That's crazy!"

"Yeah, crazy alright. Here's something else. I went to see that fight between Sheppard and McMasters. It wasn't much of a brawl because Sheppard knocked him out with just one blow."

"One blow! To McMasters?"

"A Jack Broughton uppercut and it was all over. I'll never forget it!"

Obediah's mouth dropped open. He remembered McMasters being a huge man, and the thought of him being laid out with one blow was hard to swallow. He grabbed a chair and gingerly sat down.

Fretted and apprehensive, Obediah never heard of a bare-knuckle brawler knocking out another in just one round. Chancery and grappling, even fibbing and strapping were techniques that would keep a fighter upright for several rounds. He knew Crabb's fights were short, but that was obvious. His opponents would waste their energy on useless blows, and then his prized fisticuffer would finish them off.

The Professor got up from his desk again, and began his meandering pace.

"I saw them apply a buttery substance to Sheppard's hands and face in their corner before the fight, just like you did with Will. It probably was the same salve they found in their crucible."

"The same as ours?"

"Actually, no," he said, pensively.

"I don't believe they're of the same ingredients. The behavior of the two insects were far different. I'm trying to understand the properties here. If I'm right and the two artifacts were a complete unit, why would the ancients devise two separate containers of a balming agent?"

"Ya think their salve gave Sheppard the power to knock out McMasters?" asked Obediah.

"I don't know, "answered the Professor. "It may have. It certainly wasn't snake oil!"

Frustrated, the Professor began to pace again, tugging on his ear lobe. His stride seemed expeditionary, stalking, like he was hunting a prey. After a few moments, he stopped and whirled around to face the other man.

"This is ancient Greek chemistry," he said, making holes in the air with his finger. "The proprietary ingredients, that is, the emollients and resins to produce these exotic elixirs, could date back to the age of Kronos, more than thirty-five hundred years ago."

"How could the Greeks..." began Obediah.

"It's not for us to say," quipped the scientist, flipping his hand to the side, impatiently. "They invented *Greek fire*, after all."

"Greek fire?"

"Yes, it was an incendiary weapon used in warfare against ships. Historians believe it could be ignited on contact with water. As mysterious as it was, it was depicted on ancient vases as a flame-throwing weapon by the Byzantine navy."

"Why do ya think..."

"I don't know," cut in the Professor, impatiently. "I'm just trying to form a hypothesis here."

Anxious now, the scientist's fears were beginning to surface. "By what manner can a thimbleful of pixie grease break a man's back? When it comes to blows, how do you win hands down when one gladiator clashes with a naked fist and the other campaigns with his noggin?"

"What are ya talking about?" said the exasperated manager.

The Professor jerked his arm up in a halting manner. His mind was racing now and he didn't want any interruptions.

"What if that artifact was designed for only one warrior?" the scientist mused. "What if both salves from that curio were made initially to sustain a single combatant invincibly?"

The sleuth in the man was now beginning to emerge.

"Maybe those ointments were not meant to be separated or even shared by anyone!" The Professor carefully sat down, his eyes squinted as he became immersed in thought. His chest heaved as he let out a huge sigh. "Oh boy, can this scenario even suggest...?"

"You're going too fast for me," snorted Obediah.

"I think we have to consider the spear and shield paradox," murmured the Professor.

Obediah scratched the side of his head. He knew everything about boxing, but history and science were unknowns. He didn't know a paradox from a paramecium.

"Look," the Professor gestured to Obediah, "In the ancient Greek legends, the spear represented an irresistible force. The shield would then represent an immovable object. If one had these properties together, one would be invincible."

Obediah smiled knowingly, but was lost in the whole translation.

"Don't you see?" the Professor said, impatiently. "Practical science doesn't allow this to happen. An immovable and indestructible object, representing the shield, would have to have an immeasurable amount of energy to sustain this infinite number of mass. It would be impossible to overcome the inertia from this amount of mass."

The Professor paused to let this information sink in. It was important for Obediah to understand their delicate situation.

"Yet, an irresistible and unwavering force," he continued, "which represents the spear, would also require an untold and endless amount of energy. Energy itself, can neither be created nor destroyed. It can only be transferred. The truth being, the existence of one denies the existence of the other. Yet these properties do exist collectively, we have actually seen it for ourselves!"

"Ya mean with the ant and the mosquito?" said Obediah, his voice becoming raspy.

"Yes, and similar to all your recent fights, only now it will be Crabb as the shield and Sheppard as the spear!"

Obediah felt a lump in his chest. He couldn't swallow. Something was forbidding him to

breathe. He cautiously stood up and inhaled a deep breath. After he exhaled, he meekly asked, "Who'll win such a fight?"

"Just the thought of both meeting, is unsettling," the Professor replied.

"Neither one would give up!" Obediah exclaimed. "It would be one helluva scratch out!"

"Yes, and adding to the problem, Bolton and his fighter don't realize the consequences that could happen. This could have an overwhelming ..." the Professor's words broke off.

The comprehension of such an outcome was clouding his intellectual grasp. The uncomfortable realization was now conclusive. Whatever those reckless and erstwhile Greeks concocted in that remote age, is now being released in our time, he summarized. This is for ancient warfare, when things were simple and unvarnished. Modern man can't even understand its purpose or meaning. Will Nature even choose sides, or...

"We can't manage this," blurted out the Professor. "It's a scientific absurdity, and we cannot allow this to happen! We must stop this prize fight!"

A few miles away in the town of Rivercastle, the Pugilistic Foundation was setting their sites on the championship. Hundreds of onlookers, sportsmen, and sweepstakes-charlies, were surrounding the prize ring. Gamblers and odds-makers, including the ante-up rabble, were swarming over each other.

Like any loud and boisterous athletic game, the crowd noise was at a fever pitch as colorful flags and banners fluttered about. Everyone knew this fight was for all the marbles.

Struggling through the mayhem, the Professor pressed to find his fighter. Over the heads of the clamorous throng, he could see Obediah arguing with Crabb just outside the ring. Ignoring his manager, Crabb then climbed between the ropes as the rowdy horde howled. No one gave an inkling to Obediah when he screamed to his corner-man as the two pugilists met in the center ring. The deafening uproar of the crowd overwhelmed the peal of the tinny bell that opened the first round.

Summer finally arrived in Norcrest as the noonday sun swept over the town's Mather's beach. The surf is calm and sunbathers were again sprinkled along its tiny cove. The do-nothing day was reminiscent of unpretentious bygone times.

Not far from here, stood the town of Rivercastle. No one anymore, speaks of the occurance that happened on that particular day. Where, in an extraordinary moment in time, two opponents acquired an insurmountable as well as an unattainable gift from a man called, Melankomas, and never the twain shall meet.

THE MORON

Ethan Canter

It was a warm spring day, the warmest yet, and Mr. P had decided to walk home through the park, since Nature, he knew, was the finest thing in Creation.

People had invented marvelous things, to be sure, he thought to himself, as he had many times before, but they could not have done so without Nature as their model. In fact, Mr. P reasoned, people hadn't really *created* anything, because everything was already, and firstly, present in Nature. People only re-fashioned Nature, re-arranged it, re-organized it.

Mr. P considered the bench he was presently walking past. Wood and metal, both from Nature. And the thing itself, a seat, to put it generally, that too Mr. P knew was something people had discovered in Nature – a fallen tree laid up against another still standing, rock carved and smoothed away by the power of the waves, and so on. True, none of these were the perfect seat, of course – though some were amazingly comfortable, and Mr. P did have first-hand experience of that. But the point was, he contended, that the idea of a seat was already present in Nature, people had only adapted it to their trends and fashions.

But when it came right down to it, when one had to say once and for all who *invented* The Seat, well, there was just no question, Mr. P thought – it was Nature. And anyone who suggested otherwise, he reflected, was just simply wrong, and unfortunately wrong at that, for they were missing the majesty of Nature, they were separating themselves from what they were, since, obviously, people came from Nature too. And that, Mr. P considered as he came to the edge of the park, that was Man's downfall, to separate himself from Nature. It was self-destruction, and, sadly, it was the sign of his times.

He paused outside the gates of the park and looked across the busy boulevard at the line of storefronts that faced him, and he felt sad – sad for people, sad for how they'd lost their way, sad for how they'd forgotten the old ways, sad for how they'd forgotten to live as one with Nature. "These days," he said to himself as he lit a hand-rolled cigarette, "these days it's just hard to respect people."

Just then two boys came to a skidding halt on their bicycles near Mr. P, just a few feet from the entrance to the park.

Mr. P looked down at the boys and smiled. Children are the answer, he thought. Their minds are free, and open. They live in the moment. They are, he knew, one with Nature. If children ruled the world there wouldn't be any wars, he thought, as he crossed the boulevard. And there wouldn't be a five-day workweek either, he jested to himself, though also knowing it was true. And with a smile on his face from this last thought he entered one of his many favorite drinking spots.

He waited his turn at the bar counter and then found a comfortable seat against the wall to the side of it, though still close enough to the entrance to enjoy the sight of passers-by through the establishment's front windows, as well as the blooming foliage in the park across the boulevard.

The place was really beginning to fill up now with the end of the day, indeed, the end of the week crowd.

Mr. P rolled another cigarette, crossed his legs, took a long sip from his glass and sat back, contented.

The little pleasures, he thought to himself, and looked around the place, that was what people had forgotten. What could be more human, he questioned, though of course rhetorically – what could be more natural than this, a warm and familiar spot filled with people relaxing in the company of one another, chatting, laughing, just being themselves? There were no facades here, he knew. Neckties were loosened, or just altogether removed and stuffed into a pocket or rolled up and slipped into a bag. Shirts were untucked. Top buttons were undone. And smiles and laughter weren't fake, they were real, and honest, and *natural.*

However, there was something troubling Mr. P. Something that he wished he had someone to tell about, just to get it off his chest. It was a simple trouble, to be sure. It involved the assistant he had recently taken on. In fact, the new assistant was the trouble.

Mr. P reached for his glass, but found it empty. He raised his eyebrows and grunted to himself, surprised to find his drink done already, and then, with a shrug, as if to say, "Ah well, never mind," made his way to the bar to get another.

He perused the faces at the bar, hoping to see someone he recognized. But he didn't. He lingered a little, drink in hand, waiting to see if he might strike up a conversation with a stranger, and so have someone to relate the story of his new assistant to. But this didn't happen either.

People were just so closed off these days, he thought to himself, as he took his seat against the wall again and rolled himself another cigarette. People were just so self-involved, and especially in the cities, he considered. They missed out on what life was really about.

Mr. P lit his cigarette and took a long sip of his drink.

His new assistant was self-involved too, just like these people, he thought. Then, feeling suddenly, and a bit strangely self-conscious, Mr. P looked around, thinking that perhaps the assistant might be somewhere in the crowd.

He wasn't.

Well, of course he wasn't, Mr. P thought, because the young man never went out anyway, or so he said. He was a writer, Mr. P reflected, and somewhat sarcastically. An unpublished writer, he corrected himself, if there was such a thing. That is, he considered, re-crossing his legs, to be an unpublished writer was much like being an unhatched chicken, and he laughed out loud at the thought. Indeed, he mused, who would ever conceive to call an egg an unhatched chicken? It was either an egg or a chicken. And though of course a chicken always came from an egg, an egg did not always produce a chicken.

"Ah, there is the rub," he said to himself, and reached for his glass, which, though not empty, would obviously be so soon, and so he made his way to the bar again.

The place was quite busy now and the line at the bar was long, so Mr. P decided it would make more sense to get two of his drinks at once this time, rather than have to wait in line again later.

"Just planning for the future," he said to the barmaid as she handed him his change.

"What?" she said, having not heard him over the noise at the bar.

"I'm planning for the future," Mr. P re-announced, still grinning at the humor of his statement and holding both glasses up, one in each hand, to emphasize the joke.

The barmaid smiled awkwardly and turned to serve the next customer.

People didn't even have the time to laugh anymore, Mr. P thought to himself, taking a sip from one of the glasses and making his way through the crowd back to his seat against the wall.

Halfway through rolling a fresh cigarette he reached for his glass. But then he stopped as he realized that he'd forgotten which one he'd already drank from.

With his hand poised in mid-reach, he suddenly remembered that both drinks were his anyway.

"You donkey, P," he said to himself with a laugh, and took a long sip from one of the drinks.

With the cigarette between his lips he spent some time looking through his pockets for his lighter. When he finally paused from his search to take another sip of his drink he found his lighter, which had been on the table the whole time, only blocked from view by one of his drinks.

"Well, you are in a fine state," he said good-humoredly to himself. "But, if that damned assistant had been here," he went on, wiping a little perspiration from his brow, for it had begun to get quite warm in the place. "If that little unhatched chicken were here," he said, contently amused with himself, "he would have known exactly where the lighter was, and which glass was which as well."

And it was true, he admitted, the young man was good at remembering things. But, then again, he interjected himself, he did have a tendency to take it all a little too far.

That unhatched chicken just couldn't relax, just couldn't let things be as they were, Mr. P observed. He wasn't a nervous type, not really. He was just...just – just what? Mr. P searched for the one word that really described the assistant, that really summed up the whole of his character, and which also summed up the whole of the trouble Mr. P had with him.

"Ah yes," he said aloud, remembering the word. "He was an intellectual."

But not a real intellectual, Mr. P noted. Not a true intellectual. He was one of those types who only think they're an intellectual. Even worse, one of those types who wouldn't call themselves an intellectual, who would even deny it when others pointed it out – one of those types of intellectuals, the worst type in fact, who were such intellectuals that they believed they weren't intellectuals.

Mr. P chuckled at his own witticism and raised his glass.

The truth of the matter was that the young man thought himself a writer. It was true that the young man could turn a good phrase now and then, Mr. P admitted, for he had been kind enough to read some of the assistant's work. But turning a good phrase doesn't a writer make – nor does it even make for good writing. It was only but one part of a larger whole, a much larger whole.

The problem was simply that the young man considered himself a writer, in fact even called himself a writer, but while no one else did. He was still unpublished, and not for lack of trying, Mr. P knew. Whenever one of his manuscripts was rejected – and he claimed to have numerous of them – whenever he was again denied publication he'd rail against what he referred to as the 'usurpation of art and expression by the commodificationists of mediocrity.'

Commodificationist wasn't even a word, Mr. P reflected. And therein, he thought with a strike of revelation, therein was a precise example of the chicken's problem.

Mr. P hastily reached for his tobacco and began rolling a fresh cigarette as his thought, complete with a poignant and witty metaphor, unwound itself inside his head.

The chicken knew that commodificationist wasn't a word, that was a fact. But when Mr. P had pointed this out to him, kindly of course, even cushioning it with an air of good-humor, since, to be honest, he, Mr. P, was a kind and good-hearted man, a man of Nature really, whose sole intention was to lend a hand whenever and wherever it was needed – but, yes, when he'd pointed out this fact, only with the intention of being helpful of course, the chicken had responded by saying, "I've just invented it."

It was little wonder why he wasn't published, Mr. P thought with a snort. The young man was like a chicken trying to pretend that it had not come from an egg, he concluded, celebrating his metaphor with a silent toast to himself.

To be honest, Mr. P went on, nearing the end of his second glass and beginning to feel a bit hungry – to be honest, he felt a little sorry for the chicken. It was apparent that the chicken wasn't very much liked. He rarely went out – he was always at home reading and writing, or so he said. And the few friends he did have, or claimed to have, since Mr. P had met not a one of them – his few friends, from what the little chicken had said about them, seemed to be of the same type as himself. And Mr. P laughed, though a little sadly, at the thought of the chicken, with his chicken friends, all sitting in a room, talking in their invented words, disclaiming the world, and all together pretending they didn't come from eggs – pretending even that they weren't chickens. Indeed, Mr. P chuckled, finishing his second glass with a triumphant gulp, indeed and certainly pretending they weren't chickens because they were all so convinced that they were writers.

After relieving himself in the toilet, Mr. P stopped at the bar for a departing shot of whisky. Nothing like a little nightcap for the walk home, he thought.

The warmth in his chest from the alcohol was a wonderful feeling, he noted, as he stepped outside into the evening street and drew in a deep breath of cool and fresh air.

But he seemed to draw that breath in a little too quick, or a little too deep, for it sent him into a fit of coughing that reddened his face and brought tears to his eyes.

Being absolutely opposed to spitting, since, Mr. P knew, it was the number one cause of the spread tuberculosis – not that he had tuberculosis, of course – but all the same, he swallowed down whatever it was he'd just coughed up into his mouth, then pulled out his tobacco to roll a cigarette, and began walking.

In the end, he realized, it wasn't animosity that he truly felt towards the chicken, but rather it was pity. He almost felt as though he might walk over to the chicken's place right that instant and tell him so. Or better yet, drag the poor man out for a drink. To hell with it all, he thought, they'd stuff into a taxi, drive to the center of town, visit every drinking spot they could find until it was closing time, and then they'd get a big bottle of wine and watch the sun come up in the park. They'd have a damn good time of it. They'd tear up the town. Hell, Mr. P thought with a great laugh, maybe he'd even invent a word or two himself.

Just then the sudden smell of food so distracted Mr. P that before he realized it he was inside a late-night take-away grill, ordering and paying and laughing at himself for salivating at just the scent of hot food.

Back on the street, he laughed between chews and swallows, not knowing what he was eating, as he'd forgotten what he'd ordered and was now too distracted by eating it to stop and try to decipher what it was. But what does it matter, he thought. Since whatever it was, it was damn good, and it most absolutely hit the spot. In fact, it was so good that he suddenly realized he'd finished it. He dragged the paper napkin across his face in one quick swagger and threw it and the crushed container in the trashcan at the corner.

He felt warm and full inside. He pulled out his tobacco again and began thinking of the soft and cozy bed that awaited him at home. It had been a good night after all, he thought.

When Mr. P reached his door he was already nearly half asleep. Will alone kept his eyes from falling shut as he searched his pockets for his keys. Finding them, he unlocked the door and proceeded to push it open. But the door jammed on something. That's strange, he thought. He gave the door another push, but it only skidded slightly.

Mr. P was confused and tired, and couldn't see anything in the darkness. He knelt down and reached his hand through the ajar door and felt around on the floor. Suddenly his hand found something. It felt like paper – an envelope, a large and full envelope. He gave it a tug and it came loose and the door suddenly opened.

In the hall he turned on a light and inspected the envelope. It was a large, manila envelope, and it was addressed to him. However, it hadn't been posted. It simply, and only, had his name on it, no address, no return address, no stamps.

That is odd, Mr. P thought, turning on a light in the kitchen and fixing himself a final nightcap.

With the drink in one hand and the envelope in the other, Mr. P stumbled into the living room and flopped down on the sofa.

He took a sip of the drink and inspected the envelope again. Strange, and intriguing, he thought. "Well, nothing like a little mystery to end the night," he said to himself, putting his drink down on the small table beside him.

He pulled out his tobacco for his customary end-of-the-night cigarette, but, also, somehow, simultaneously tried to open the envelope at the same time. The result was what Mr. P called a right old mess. Tobacco spilled all over his lap and onto the sofa, and the contents of the envelope, which seemed to be an abundance of loose sheets of paper, slipped and slid and skidded across the living room floor.

"What a state you're in, old son," Mr. P said to himself with a laugh, and collected up the tobacco and put it back into its pouch. Then he reached down and gathered up the sheets of paper, which, he now noticed, were all covered in typescript. That really is bizarre, he thought to himself.

As he rolled his cigarette he glanced at the disheveled pile of paper now beside him on the sofa. His eyes floated to the bottom of one of the pages and there he noticed a page number.

With his cigarette lit and hanging from between his lips, he gathered up the papers again and began to sort them.

The task done, and the collated pile resting on his lap, Mr. P ashed his cigarette, though just shy of the ashtray. It fell and crumbled on the table. He took another sip from his drink, and with a determined inhale of smoke, which he didn't exactly exhale, but simply let fall and roll out of his nostrils, set himself to inspecting the strange pile of typewritten pages.

Without address or title or designation of any kind, other than the page numbering, the document dove straight into telling its tale. Squinting, as it was quite late now and the lamplight in the room was rather dim, Mr. P read the first line, which ran: 'It was a warm spring day, the warmest yet, and Mr. P had decided to walk home through the park, since Nature, he knew, was the finest thing in Creation.'

Indeed, Mr. P thought, Nature certainly was that.

He read the next line, which ran: 'People had invented marvelous things, to be sure, he thought to himself, as he had many times before, but they could not have done so without Nature as their model.'

"Well, I say," Mr. P exclaimed to himself, reaching for his drink and again unsuccessfully ashing his cigarette. "I do believe the little chicken has laid an egg." He chuckled at his quaint witticism. And a bit of a golden egg at that, too, he thought, proudly staring down at his own name in black print.

He leaned a little more comfortably into the sofa and took the story up in both hands this time.

Yes, it really had been a good evening after all, he thought, and began to read the story again from the beginning. But before he'd gotten through the first paragraph his eyes fell shut, his hands let go the pages, his head dropped off to one side, and he began to snore.

THE MOTHERS

Zackary Medlin

It didn't take long for Knoxville to shrink to nothing in the rearview. Tara and Josh were quiet, each waiting for the other to say something. Something easy, something that would wipe away the thing they couldn't talk about: Tara was pregnant. But today wasn't going to be easy. She turned off I-75 onto the old state highway, a two-lane ribbon of asphalt parting the sea of tupelos and black oak. The road seemed to mark a delineation in time. All vestiges of modernity faded from memory and were replaced with a deeper knowing–the land's memory. Something so lush with malice light struggled to breathe in it.

Tara had given up trying to relax her jaw and had, instead, turned to simply ignoring the ache pulsing in her back teeth as she stared down the vein of blacktop running through Old

Tennessee. She didn't notice herself accelerating. Didn't notice herself not looking at Josh. She wouldn't look at him again until they arrived at her grandmother's.

Grandma Collin's house, like much of the region, was a place outside of time. Speckles of black mildew had begun to climb up the clapboard siding and splotches of gray-green lichen had begun to build up on the old cedar shake shingles. The signs of age only worked to further cement it in some distant past. The front door was open to allow the house to breathe. A tidy foyer was visible through the screen door. The mesh gave it a grainy look, like an old photograph.

As Tara and Josh walked toward the porch, his hand brushed hers. She took hold of it, almost out of habit, but his hand was warm, and isn't every habit a comfort? Tara took a few more steps before letting go. When the couple reached the stairs to the porch, she leaned into him a little. Josh wrapped an arm around her. She whispered to him to let her do the talking, and for him to not say anything too stupid trying to sound smart.

"Meemaw, it's me!" The screen door slammed behind Tara with a sharp wood-on-wood clap. There was something almost comforting about the sound of the door and the tone in Tara's voice. Something childlike, as if crossing the threshold into grandma's house, any grandma's house, demanded a certain quantity of joy as toll. Josh entered, catching the door behind him to prevent it from slamming again, almost like he was trying to stay outside the moment. Or maybe it was out of fear. This sort of door, the old kind, can only open so many times before something starts to splinter when it closes.

Grandma Collins squeezed by Tara to approach Josh, "Oh my, would you look at those eyes, blue as robins' eggs." She extended her prim, dainty hand to Josh, palm down, "It's my pleasure to meet anyone that can make my little girl smile."

Josh gave her hand a polite faux kiss. "Oh, the pleasure's all mine."

Grandma Collins glanced over her shoulder to Tara, "Finally got you a good one, Tater." She ushered the couple towards the small living room before disappearing into the kitchen. "I'll get us a little something to nibble on."

"Tater?" Josh raised an eyebrow.

"Yep. Meemaw calls me Tater." Tara furrowed her brow and leaned in closer to him, "*Meemaw* calls me Tater." She said it through a tight-lipped scowl, a warning, really, but there was a flicker in her eyes that had been missing earlier in the day. And, for a moment, they both felt something that had been missing. "I'm going to go help Meemaw; knowing her, she's probably in there trying to throw together a whole last-minute brunch.

In the kitchen, Grandma Collins was at the counter and staring out the window. More accurately, she was staring out, that a window happened to be in front of her was of no consequence, though she had learned it made others more comfortable. She busied her hands slicing the crusts off a cucumber sandwich. Next to her was a plate loaded with a neat pyramid of finger sandwiches.

Tara approached and tried to grab a slice of cucumber from the cutting board, only to have her hand slapped away. Grandma Collins broke off her stare but continued to slice away at the last sandwich, the capstone for the full plate beside her. Tara sidled up next to her and picked at one of the strips of crust littering the cutting board.

"Meemaw, I'm in trouble." She fidgeted with the crust until it was little more than a pile of crumbs. "I'm in *trouble* trouble."

Grandma Collins set the knife on the counter and placed her hand on Tara's belly. "I know, Tater; I know. We'll talk after lunch. I'm sure it's been a drive for you to get here."

"I just couldn't have you looking at me anymore without knowing." Tara seemed to shrink into herself as she said it. "I need help. We don't have the money to have it taken care of, especially since they banned it here. We'd have to go out of state to find a clinic."

"That's how you plan to handle it?" There was no judgment in her voice, nor was it really a question.

"Josh says it's for the best."

Grandma Collins picked up the plate and turned to head back toward the living room. "Come on, it's getting hot; these sandwiches won't keep long."

Grandma Collins placed the plate in the center of the small coffee table while Tara poured sweet tea. As Grandma Collins took her seat, Josh reached a hand towards a sandwich, only to have it grabbed by her.

"Do us the honors, Tater." With her other hand, Grandma Collins took hold of Tara's hand, who, in turn, reached for Josh. With the circle closed, the two women bowed their heads and Tara began saying Grace.

Josh, too, bowed his head. An electric pain stabbed behind his eyes. When he clenched them shut, white-hot bursts of lightning exploded against the dark. It was involuntary how hard he squeezed Grandma Collins's hand, but she didn't flinch or pull away. Instead, she returned the squeeze, harder, until he could feel her nails cutting into his soft palm. A final explosive light burst open before him like a milky eye with a hungry rectangular pupil.

Josh jolted away and awake, like a hypnic jerk on the edge of sleep.

Tara closed the prayer, and Josh mumbled an "Amen" as his hands were released. He glanced at his palm. No blood. No nail marks. The pain remained, but only as an afterimage. A thought of pulverized bones slithered up his arms and settled in his chest.

Tara held a napkin out to Josh. "Ew, here, your palms are *super* sweaty. I apologize for that, Meemaw. He can be kind of–"

Grandma Collins cut her off, "Hush, leave the boy alone; he's nervous is all. It's the first time he's meeting your family. You know how scary I can be." She bared her teeth and made a show of pulling a mean face, and then bit viciously into a cucumber sandwich held daintily between thumb and forefinger.

"Has Tater told you much about our family? We're about as Old South as you can get. You can trace our family back to Vardy. You heard of it? A witchy place, made up of exiled Germans, Indians, and runaway slaves marrying and mixing all the magics they carried. You know, they say Tara's momma had the sight."

"Mama didn't–" was as far as Tara got before Grandma Collins rose from her chair and cut in.

"Hold that thought. You keep eating, I'm going to go see if I can't wrangle us up some dessert. I can throw together an ambrosia salad if nothing else. Tater, give me a hand, won't you?"

Grandma Collins paused in the doorway to the kitchen, carefully balancing the dishes she carried. "You know, if you want to really learn about our family, the two of you should head up to Varny. Go call on Granny Mabel."

"Granny Mabel?" Tara didn't know the name, but she knew they had family spread wide across eastern Tennessee. "Is she kin to us?"

"She's ain't blood, but she's kin."

Once in the kitchen, Grandma Collins placed the plates into the sink and turned the water on. She let it run as she turned to Tara and took hold of her hands. "It's okay, Tater. You're making the right choice. I don't have enough to get you to no out-of-state clinic, but I do have this," Grandma Collins pressed something cold and metal into Tara's palm, a pendant on a fine chain. "Go see Granny Mabel. She knows the old ways. Give this to her and she'll help you take care of it"

Tara looked at the necklace in her hand. It was a crucifix, but more. Branches and leaves sprung from the top and crossbeam, and roots grew from the base. It was as if Christ was being lifted up as a part of a living cross. He wasn't emaciated or anguished, either, though he did have Thomas's slit in his belly. Otherwise, he was full-bodied, almost soft to the touch.

"But Meemaw, it's a sin, ain't it? One God can't look away from."

"Shush. You ask Granny Mabel about all that. She'll tell you how it goes; she's the most God-fearing women I've ever known."

Tara choked on her own breath as she tried to speak, shattering any words that were beginning to take shape in her throat. Grandma Collins pulled Tara in tight, wrapped her in her arms, and whispered, "Listen to me, Tater. You ain't the first woman to fall, and you won't be the last. But you got family to catch you. We'd all be better off if Lilith had stayed around to catch Eve. Weren't really fair, was it, having only Adam? Off naming everything, like birds and animals don't know what they are." Grandma Collins lifted her eyes to the door separating the kitchen from the living room, and Josh. "Going around thinking he did something when all he did was learn what was already there. Go see Granny Mabel. Y'all can pray on it."

Grandma Collins turned the water off and took the key lime pie she'd made last night out of the fridge. It was Tara's favorite.

Tara strangled the steering wheel as the Camry wound its way through the narrow mountain road leading up to Vardy, but it wasn't the drive clenching her fist. The drive was slow going, now; the road demanded a more focused, deliberate pace, but her mind raced faster and faster as the distance between her and Vardy shrank. The surrounding forest's thick canopy reached out over the road like an overpass, forming a green tunnel blocking out the midday sun so that only occasional droplets of light were able to drip down on the road. The rare slants of light only heightened her tension, as if the weight of the whole thing was cracking and threatening to collapse on them at any moment.

Tara's hand found its way to her chest and began to fidget with the pendant. "I know you don't believe in all this: Granny Witches and folk magic."

"I didn't know you did either."

"I don't. I know mamma wasn't a witch and she didn't have 'the sight.' She had schizophrenia and a drug problem. Oxycontin, then fentanyl, then.... It's a problem up here, you know? It's a problem everywhere, but here it's something more. So maybe they need something more to believe in, too."

The pitted asphalt road devolved into rough gravel, then to dirt. Up ahead, a derelict shack bordered the dirt road. Josh stared into the inky void that filled the space behind the cracked and missing windows. The front door lay locked away behind a sheet of plywood spray-painted with the word CLOSED.

"It's not magic; of course, it's not magic. But what does it matter what you call it if it works? And we are going to these people *for help.* So, you better fucking hope it works." Tara's hand returned to the pendant, pinching it and rubbing her thumb in small tight circles. She didn't remember putting it on, hadn't even realized she was wearing it, but she was glad to now feel its weight against her neck, the metal warming beneath her fingers.

"I'm sorry, I—I ramble when I'm uncomfortable, and everything makes me uncomfortable. I didn't even want to—I'm not sure I should be..." He trailed off, ashamed. "I'm just scared."

Tara brought the car to a dead stop and stared *into* Josh. "*I'm* the one doing this, and *I'm* scared, too. This is crazy. But what choice do we have? The nearest clinic's in Virginia. We're broke. Hell, we had to borrow Jessie's car just to get here." Tears welled in her eyes. "But you're here, Josh. And I need you here." She blinked her tears away and slid her hand down to the shifter. The car lurched back into motion. "If nothing else, I need you here to get me home."

A ragged wooden sign marking the outskirts of Vardy was chiseled into roughhewn boards nailed to a splintered stump of tree. Tara and Josh pulled into the store across from the sign and parked at one of the two gas pumps out front. Josh fiddled with the pump while Tara made her way inside. He walked over to the sign while the tank filled. He ran his fingers over small symbols carved into the wood. They were unknown to Josh, but not totally devoid of recognition. As his finger dragged over the splintery edges of the symbols, he felt something like an itch in his memory. It felt like looking at old photographs, like Victorian *memento mori* daguerreotypes of dead children or the grainy black-and-gray newsprint images of Civil Rights protests—the fanged, violent ones. Dead moments kept alive against their will by the pain and fear and hatred filling them. He jerked his hand away from the sign, taking a fragment of it with him. The splinter pierced deep into the fleshy pad of his middle finger and embedded itself beneath the surface. He watched as a rusty circle swelled around the sliver, a bead of blood too small to leave the skin.

Inside, Tara browsed an aisle of candles bearing the images of saints and goddesses, occasionally leaning in to smell one. Willowy dreamcatchers fluttered on the arms of a spinner rack as Josh came through the door. He joined her on the candle aisle and picked up a candle with a portrait of a young woman. Two pink roses bloomed from where her eyes should be, and petals fell like tears.

"That's Flora, the flower goddess."

Tara and Josh both jumped at the voice that materialized behind them and turned to see the dark-skinned boy in his early teens who had appeared. The plastic name tag pinned to his t-shirt read "Kyrin."

"The Wiccan girls like it; I think it's because it smells like patchouli. She's not just about flowers, either; Flora's the fertility goddess, too."

Josh put the candle down a touch too fast for it to seem natural as Tara side-stepped away from him.

"We got crystals, Indian Medicine bags, more saints, and some sinners, too" The boy gestured to the bottom row of candles. "All them are Voodoo saints. The hippie witches don't seem to really care where things come from; they just mix and match the smells they like."

"You know none of this is real." Jay took a whiff of another candle, this one bearing a portrait of a woman and bore the name "Lilith." It smelled like patchouli, too.

"Course, it ain't. Just what we sell white folks. Wanna buy it?" The boy smiled and wiggled his eyebrows up and down, then turned to walk back to the counter. "We got loads of weird white ladies showing up since they had that witchy shit on TV. Travel Channel or History Channel or some shit."

"We're looking for Granny Mabel." Tara's voice cut through the store, loud and taut, like a guitar string tuned to high.

The boy stopped mid-step and looked back at the young woman. "Guess you do know a little something after all." He rounded the corner of the counter and came to a stop next to the cash register. He leaned on the countertop, supporting himself with his elbows and resting his chin in his hands. "Hey, Sherri! We got a girl up here wanting Granny Mabel," he shouted while staring down Josh. "You sure about the abortion?" He said it to Josh but cut his eyes over to Tara and his face broke into a toothy grin. Silence filled the store as the boy waited for a response. "Most ain't got the daddy with 'em when they get here. So, I guess that tells on you, too. Not man enough to—ow, fucking shit!"

A slender hand twisted the boy's ear, yanking him head-first towards the door behind the counter. When he got close enough, the hand let go of his ear. The owner of the hand—a lithe woman in a flowing floral dress and loose black sweatshirt—slapped the back of his head. Hard. "Don't speak on things you don't know nothing about, little boy." She turned her eyes to Tara and let them fall to the necklace around Tara's neck. "I apologize for my brother; he'll understand in time. Or, maybe he won't, if he's lucky. I'm Sherri."

The boy sulked his way through the door behind the counter and yanked it closed behind him. Josh sulked his way down the aisles, browsing the wall of coolers in the back of the store. He glanced back at the counter as he grabbed a Miller Tall Boy. The women were leaning in towards each other; Tara's hands were in Sherri's. When he saw them pull away from each other, he began walking towards the counter. Sherri scribbled down something on an old receipt and folded it into Tara's hand. Tara stuffed it in a pocket and turned towards Josh.

"I'll be in the car." Her voice is quiet, muffled by all the space between them.

Josh nodded and set the beer on the counter and reached for his wallet.

Sherri reached for the can, "This going to do it for you?"

"Unless you got something stronger. Whiskey...Xanex?" Josh smiled a half smile at his joke, one that seemed to apologize for itself.

Sherri hesitated. Her eyes drifted to the window and watched as Tara climbed into the driver seat. Sherri reached below the counter and produced a thin pint bottle. The murky brown glass hid the contents, but not the smell. With one hand, she pushed the beer can to the side with the liquor bottle. With her other hand, she pushed his wallet away. She leaned across the counter, looked him in the eyes, and whispered, "The boy was right about you, you know. Just ain't right to say it out loud." She looked back to Tara sitting alone in the car. "Poor girl is struggling enough."

Josh backed out of the store, unable to break eye contact with Sherri, no matter how hard he tried. When he felt the door's metal push bar press into his back, he spun through the door and walked away.

In the car, Josh asked what Sherri had said to her.

"She told me I don't need to be afraid, and that no matter what happens, it'll be okay." Tara checks the address on the receipt. "I think she's been to see her, too."

Josh brought his hand to his mouth and bit at the splinter in his finger; it seemed to slither deeper into his flesh. It had started to throb, steady as a pulse.

Time on Maypole Drive was a molasses-thick flow, black and bitter, but Granny Mabel's house was an island rising out of this stream. However, the house was not impervious to the passing decades. One imagines it must have once been vibrant, that its pink siding must have blushed like a prized rose bush. It had since wilted into a dirty pastel smeared across the clapboards. Still, this only served to make it soft, almost inviting. The small yard surrounding it was frequently mistaken as an untamed tangle of weeds, the same as most yards on the one-lane dirt road. One could hardly be blamed for not recognizing the jasmine, angel's trumpets, and tuberose. Few ventured into the yard after dark, and the streetlights on Maypole Drive had lost their light long ago, so few ever saw these flowers in bloom alongside the other carefully cultivated moon flowers, daturas, and night-scented orchids that overran the flowerboxes beneath each window.

The front door to Granny Mabel's house was painted a deep burgundy, and Tara and Josh could see from the street that it had been left ajar, like a wound opening into the house. Josh swigged from the pint Sherri had given him while Tara reread the address written on the slip of receipt. It was still the same as it had been every other time she had read it while sitting in front of the house.

Feeling the neighbors' stares fall on her finally dragged Tara out of the amber moment she had sunk into. She crumpled the receipt, tossed it into the floorboard on Josh's side, and opened the car door and began the walk to the door.

Tara let her fingers brush the tops of the flora lining the walkway to the house. Josh followed closely behind. Tara knocked lightly, which pushed the door open a bit wider. She called out and peeked into the house while she waited for some response. It was dark inside, but a murky aura seemed to seep from the lush walnut floors and the walls decorated in rich reds. The combination made the atmosphere inside feel somehow organic, and the air denser—so thick that Tara began to wonder if her words had been allowed to travel through it at all.

"Yes, child. Come in." An old woman's voice, thin and reedy, like a freshly rosined bow had drawn the words from a viola, soft but not fragile. "Sherri said you'd be calling."

As Tara made her way down the hall towards the voice, she realized how bright and warm the house actually felt. The walls and floor seemed to glow, filling the space with their own dark light.

Josh had yet to cross the threshold into Granny Mabel's. The door knocker had snagged his eye. The strike plate was a tree encircled by a brass ring; the knocker hung from a hinge in the center of the tree, a simple inverted T. It was familiar. His fingers traced the outline while he tried to place the symbol. He grabbed the knocker and lifted it up so that the crossbar of the T spanned the top of the circle. The underside of the knocker had Christ etched into it. He realized where he had seen it before. It was like an elaborate, fleshed-out form of the angular symbol carved into the welcome sign. He jerked his hand back as if a new splinter had dug into his skin. The knocker fell against the strike plate with a sharp, brassy clap. The throbbing in his finger had moved up behind his right eye. He took another swig of liquor to try and wash the headache away. When he entered the house, Josh he fumbled forward through the thick dark, reaching a hand, feeling for a wall to guide him as his eyes adjusted.

Granny Mabel turned her clouded, sightless eyes towards the doorway as Tara approached the room "Don't worry, child. You don't got to be afraid. Can't nothing bad happen to you here." The old woman reached a frail hand out to Tara, and with the other, she patted the sofa.

Tara took a seat next to Granny Mabel and took hold of the old woman's hand. Granny Mabel's touch reminded Tara of autumn, like rust-red leaves rustling on dry branches. Her skin was thin, like wrinkled rice paper, and every bone and joint was visible beneath the surface. But her grip was still oak-strong.

Granny Mabel released Tara's hand and leaned forward to grab a rumpled soft pack of Marlboros from the coffee table. She shook a cigarette out and pulled a lighter from the cellophane around the pack. She lit the cigarette, inhaled deeply, then let the smoke drift from her nose and mouth in milky clouds that mimicked the cataracts crowding out her eyes. "Boy, you're going to be needed here, too." She took another drag from the cigarette.

Josh peeked around the doorway. Granny Mabel gestured with her head towards a high-back chair in the corner of the room. He took a seat and tried, and failed, to avoid the old woman's gaze. He closed his own eyes and concentrated on the little bit of alcohol running through him. It was the only warmth he could find in the house.

Granny Mabel ashed her cigarette in a small amber-glass ashtray on the coffee table. The area around it was immaculate; she never missed. She turned her attention back to Tara. "I can feel your nerves, baby girl. I know what they say out there about us. That we witches and heathens. That we ungodly. Been saying it since Salem. Weren't no truth to it then, even less to it now. We a holy folk." She took a final drag from her cigarette and stubbed it out.

"Caleb, fetch me the family bible." She said it to the center of the room in a voice that seemed louder than what her compact body could possibly contain. Loud, but not a shout. Rather, the words seemed to simply roll through the house like an ocean swell rippling towards the shore.

After a moment, a giant of a man appeared in the doorway holding a massive leather-bound tome on a pillow. The rough-cut deckled edge was yellowed, and dozens of loose slips of paper were folded between the pages. The cover had once been gilded, but only occasional flecks of gold leaf remained. He placed the pillow on Granny Mabel's lap. She nodded toward a console table on the far wall and began flipping through the bible. The margins were filled with notes and drawings.

"What magic we have, it's here." She tapped a page. An old photograph was taped above the verse: a grainy black-and-white image of trees, a cypress. A sign was nailed to the trunk. A yard or so above the sign, two dark-skinned feet dangled, bound at the ankles. They led up to a man's torso, his arms pulled behind his back. The rest of the body is cut off by the photo's edge. "Was a time people was less welcoming here. But they came around." Granny Mabel ran her fingers across the photo, letting it come to rest on the man's torso, where his heart would have been. "Whatever town or village you enter, search there for some worthy person and stay at their house until you leave..." Her eyes were closed, but she was scanning her finger from left to right, as if reading, "I am sending you out like sheep among wolves..."

Caleb returned with a tray carrying a cast-iron kettle, a stone mortar and pestle, and an earthen mug. It rattled as he placed it before Tara, despite his best efforts. Granny Mabel fell silent for a moment, then slowly blinked open her eyes and offered Tara a warm grin. "This here," she tapped the bible, "might as well be a grimoire, it's full of magic." She placed the bible and pillow between her and Tara and leaned forward to reach for the kettle. "And this, here, is tea." She smiled as she filled the mug and placed it into Tara's hands.

"Don't drink that. We don't know what's in that tea, what it'll do." Josh tried to stand but wobbled back down into his chair. On his second try, he was able to cross the room to sit next to Tara. "We should at least talk about it some more before, you know, it's too late."

"Don't you worry, boy; this ain't it yet." Granny Mabel's voice was sweet, but there was an edge to it, like maple syrup dripping from a straight razor. "This just some chamomile and valerian root. We still got lots to talk about, me and her. But that's me and her. You have your own job to do in all of this."

Josh felt Caleb's immense shadow fall over him.

"Caleb, take the boy out to the garden to gather what we need. You know the herbs and roots, right?"

Caleb nodded and put a meaty hand on Josh's shoulder.

"The boy's got to do the picking, though. Remember that. You just there to point him the way."

Caleb lifted Josh to his feet.

"Now, wait a sec." Josh tried to pull away from the massive man's grasp but only managed to stumble; he would have fallen to the ground, were it not for Caleb's grip on him. "I'm not going anywhere," his words were slurred. He realized that, beneath the burn, he'd never tasted any liquor like what Sherri had given him.

"Hush, boy. What we got to talk about ain't for menfolk. 'Sides you done part of the work to get her here, time to do your part to get her out." She turned back to Tara and her voice was all maple, no edge. "Now, I believe you have something for me."

Tara gulped down a sip of tea. "Oh, I forgot." She placed her mug on the table and removed the necklace from around her neck. "Meemaw, I mean Viola Collins, she gave me this to give to you. Forgot I was even wearing it." She placed the pendant in Granny Mabel's palm and turned to Josh. "Go on, it's okay. Just give us a minute to talk, please."

Caleb's grip on Josh's shoulder was growing more insistent. Granny Mabel looked to Caleb and raised an eyebrow. He pulled Josh towards the doorway, and with his other hand, he fished the pint bottle from Josh's back pocket and slid it into his own. Then the two men disappeared down the hall.

Granny Mable picked up the pillow holding the family bible and sidled over to sit closer to Tara. She flipped through it, pointing out the occasional verses and the prayers scribbled in the margins, "This one's a spell for a bountiful harvest." She flipped some more pages, "This one's to protect a husband or son in wartime." Her fingers found a well-worn page, the margins filled with words and symbols in a variety of languages and scripts. "And this one's for us."

Tara ran her fingers over the bible page. Her stomach clenched, and she felt tears well in her eyes. "This can't be right, though, can it? It goes against the bible, doesn't it? Against God." Tara dragged a finger down the margins. "I mean, all this is from man, but this," she placed her palm over the scripture, "This is His word." The knots in her stomach spasmed and her mouth ran dry.

"No, child." Granny Mabel's voice was tender and wrapped around Tara like a blanket. She grabbed Tara's index finger and ran it over the margins again. "This ain't from man, this is from the Mothers, all the daughters of God."

Caleb returned, alone. He placed a single pale blue robin's egg in Granny Mabel's palm.

Tara doubled over, sobbing and clutching her belly. "I can't kill it. I can't do it. It's a *sin*." She curled up fetal on the couch and rocked herself.

"This ain't no sin, child, you ain't killing nothing. The Mothers seen and heard what the soul wants and got you here to me."

Tara rolled from the couch onto all fours and began tugging at Granny Mabel's skirt, pleading through her sobs. "I changed my mind! I'll go to hell. I don't–" Tara's words were cut off by black vomit erupting from her mouth. She collapsed to the ground clutching her belly and choking out the thick ichor.

Granny Mabel nods toward Tara's empty mug of tea. "Ain't no taking it back, girl. You're just scared is all, 'cause of what all them preachers been telling you your whole life. But the Mothers heard you and know what you want. It ain't yours no more. That one's going back to God to find a different way here."

Granny Mabel leaned down closer to Tara and grabbed her hand. She held it as gently as if she was holding a baby bird. Her voice was like a cool water compress placed on Tara's fevered brow.

"You're gonna be okay, child, but there ain't no taking it back. Not now," Granny Mabel opened Tara's hand and smashed the robin's egg in her palm. "It's too late." Granny turned back to the bible on her lap as Tara spasmed on the floor, sobbing to Jesus. Granny began reading, her voice loud and taut, as to let her words rise above Tara's incoherent prayers: "If there happens to be a bird's nest in front of you along the road, in any tree or on the ground, with young ones or eggs and the hen sitting on the young or on the eggs, you are not to take the hen with the young. You must certainly let the hen go, but the young you may take for yourself so that it may go well with you and you may prolong your days!"

Tara collapsed to the floor, trembling. Granny Mabel's prayer ushered her from consciousness.

Crickets trilled all around, and the stars blinked in and out of existence. No, not stars, fireflies. The muggy air thrummed with an insectoid buzzing that scratched its way inside Tara's skull and crowded out all thoughts. She was only her senses. A rich blend of earthy notes and sulfurous undertones filled her nose, a smell so cloying and thick it felt as if she were breathing through damp cheesecloth. Her tongue was swollen, and a vegetal taste filled her mouth, as if it were coated in some bitter lichen. Her throat burned still from the bile in her vomit. Tara sat in a hardwood chair, her back held flat against the chairback. Her hands, knees, and feet were bound to the arms and legs of the chair, the leather straps pulled so tight she could feel the grain of the damp, swollen wood against the tender skin of her wrists. Her knees were bound in a way that kept her legs spread. She felt the edges of rough-hewn boards on her inner thighs. Stirrups, she realized.

Tara had been dressed in flowing white linen while she was unconscious. At first, she mistook it for a hospital gown, but as her vision cleared, she saw it was more like a baptismal robe that had been hiked up above her waist. The front of it was marred by a black stain spread across her lap.

In front of her, the surface of a stagnant pool rippled with water striders while the air above teemed with mosquitoes and dragonflies. The pond was ringed by a shore flush with life, luscious night-blooming flowers opening and closing as if inhaling the evening. Near the shore, thick roots emerged from the water and came together to form the trunk of a broad cypress. A small staircase shaped from the gnarled and bent branches of a living sapling led up to the cypress, and to Josh. He was bound to the tree, arms spread wide, as if crucified. A shape began to take form in Tara's mind, a memory just out of touch.

Josh's shirt had been removed and his chest was carved with an intricate star-like sigil. Dried blood crusted his chin, and neck. There was a glint of something round and metallic in his mouth. It was Tara's pendant, now made into a gag. The leather strap was pulled so tight it had cut into the corners of his mouth, threatening to tear his cheeks into a grisly smile. His head lolled, and he occasionally let out a gurgling whimper. A slimy rust-colored lump of flesh lay on the steps beneath his feet. His tongue.

"It's almost done, child." Granny Mabel's voice whispered into Tara's ear as the old woman appeared from behind her. She held the hand of another young woman in fresh white robes. Sherri. "The Mother's coming tonight." She ushered Sherri towards the black water. "See, God ain't no he. Why would she be? We the ones doing the making."

Granny Mabel returned from the water's edge and was met by Caleb, bearing the family bible still on its pillow. "A bible ain't nothing but our spells, 'cause men can't read no real magic." Granny Mabel flipped through the bible, found a page, and then placed it in Sherri's open hands. "You'll know when."

Tara tried to talk, to pray, to say *anything*, but found nothing but gray wisps of matter refusing to coalesce into any rational thought. All of reality seemed to ripple at the periphery.

Granny Mabel knelt before Tara and reached her hands between her bound legs. She returned to her feet holding an earthen bowl filled with black ichor. She handed the bowl to Caleb and then turned to loosen Tara's restraints. Granny

Mabel gave Tara's knee a pat, "There you go, hon. We don't need these no more."

Tara struggled to kick at the woman, to grasp at her, but her body failed her. It took all of her strength, but she managed to spit in Granny Mabel's face.

Granny Mabel spat right back into Tara's face. "Eeye for an eye. That's God's way, ain't it?" There was no malice in her voice. She and Caleb walked towards Josh and climbed the stairs leading to him. Granny took the bowl from Caleb, who then reached around to loosen the gag. The pendant hung limp against Josh's throat while Caleb took hold of the boy's face and forced his mouth into a gaping O.

Sherri began to read from the bible: "I will give you a new heart and put a new spirit in you; I will remove from you your heart of stone and give you a heart of flesh. And I will put my Spirit in you and move you to follow my decrees and be careful to keep my laws."

Granny Mabel brought the bowl to Josh's lips and began pouring the thick fluid down his throat as she took up voice alongside Sherri, "I will increase the fruit of the trees and the crops of the field." The old woman produced a small grapefruit spoon from her apron, "So that you will no longer suffer disgrace among the nations because of famine." She dug the spoon behind Josh's left eye. He spasmed and gurgled as she twisted and scooped the orb into her palm. Then she turned her attention to the right eye.

The smoky strands of thoughts in Tara's mind finally coalesced into a unified form, that of a single, uncontainable scream.

Granny Mabel dangled an eyeball above the stagnant water. "Caleb, it's time." She released one eye and let it plunge into the water. The other eye she took into her own mouth. She closed her eyes in pleasure as she chewed. A thin trail of vitreous humor dribbled from the corners of her smile.

Caleb marched toward Tara. She sat shaking, rocking, and still screaming impotently into the night. He threw her over his shoulder and walked toward the pool. Her scream was finally silenced when he dropped her into the water and held her head beneath the surface.

An instinctual rage flooded Tara, and it was that rage, that gathered her body back under her control. She thrashed, kicked, and clawed. Her nails tore through Caleb's cold flesh, but the man never flinched. His grasp on her was dispassionate but determined. Tara saw the shadows creeping in on her periphery, felt the black water fighting its way into her throat. She closed her eyes and let her body fall limp.

On the edge of perception, Tara felt a current rising from beneath her, then a rush of water bubbled against her closed eyes. Caleb took hold of her hair and lifted her head from the water. The surface of the pond roiled. Sherri closed the bible, set it aside, and waded into the pool. The surface grew more viscous with each sputtering bubble.

Then, the water fell away.

Tara stared into an undulating glob of oily black. Its surfaced roiled and gurgled. Each bubble burst to reveal an eye staring back into her. The center of the massive churning body opened to reveal a large rectangular pupil. Tara felt herself being drawn into the eye, and she let herself be swallowed. A tornado of teeth coiled around her in the vacuum of the pupil, and she was devoured, left floating in this space where each tooth became a star in a galaxy spiraling away from her. The massive black hole swirling in the center of the galaxy gazed at her the way a mother might gaze at her newborn child. Tara understood, she remembered her bible. It was Ezekiel, that was the book they read. She knew it, too, and began to mouth the verse into the void: "Their entire bodies, including their backs, their hands, and their wings, were completely full of eyes." Ezekiel had seen the angels. The Mother blinked and Tara felt it fall warm against her forehead like a kiss.

Tara turned from The Mother and gazed at a blissful Sherri, whose stare was transfixed on the angel. Tara looked at Josh, blood ran down his cheeks like tears from his emptied eye sockets. He raised his head. Tara felt as if he, too, was staring into her. He began to spasm and thrash. Something twitched and squirmed in the holes where his eyes once were. Something was crawling out. A thin pale stem wormed its way from his right eye. A second followed from the other socket. The stems began to branch and bud. Josh battered his head against the tree. A thick, gore-slick branch erupted from his mouth like a black scream and his body went limp. He continued to branch and bloom until he was naught but ragged bits of flesh dangling from the branches like autumn leaves gone to rust and waiting to fall.

As the tree's canopy spread above, blood dripped down on Tara, Sherri, and Granny Mabel. Tara noticed something in the leaves glinting in the moonlight. Sherri reached up and removed a silver apple from the branch. She bit deeply into the fruit and let the juices run free down her face, her neck, her chest. With her other hand, she cradled her own belly, which grew round and bulged against her gown.

Granny Mabel approached Tara. The deep-set wrinkles around her mouth had filled in, and black streaks now ran through her iron-gray hair. The clouds in her eyes parted to reveal clear blue irises. Robin's egg blue. She took hold of Tara's hands. "You lost something tonight, something you might not ever get back. But you know, now, what women sometimes got to do to catch each other." Granny Mabel turned Tara to face Sherri, who was still standing ankle-deep in the pond, glistening in the moonlight. "One day, another pendant might find its way back to you. If it do, you help that girl. That's the way of it. You one of us or you ain't."

Caleb approached and held the bible out to Granny Mabel. She opened the front cover and gestured to a list of women's names: Constance Maypole, Virginia Maple, Clara Maybell, Hattie Mabel. All but one had a line struck through it. Caleb offered Granny Mabel a pen. She scratched a line through Hattie Mabel and wrote *Tara* beneath it. She offered Tara the pen.

"You get to choose."

Tara took the pen in her trembling hand. Her whole body shook with soft sobs. Finally, she scribbled something on the page.

Granny Mabel looked at the page and smiled. “Myrtle, like the tree. It’s pretty.” She closed the bible and held it out to Tara.

CONTRIBUTORS

Jason Lairamore is a writer of science- fiction, fantasy, and horror who lives in Oklahoma with his beautiful wife and their three monstrously marvelous children. He is a 2023 Baen Fantasy Adventure Award finalist. He has also won Writer of the Future honors with fifteen honorable mentions, one silver honorable mention, and a semi-finalist placement. His work is both featured and forthcoming in over 100 publications to include *Neo-Opsis, New Myths, Stupefying Stories,* and *Third Flatiron* publications, to name a few.

TS S. Fulk, a neurodiverse English teacher and textbook author, lives with his neurodiverse family in Sweden. After getting a B.A. in Music and M.A.T. Secondary Education: English from Kent State University and an M.A. in English literature from the University of Toronto, he taught English in Prague, CZ before settling down in Sweden. Besides teaching and writing, TS S. Fulk is an active musician playing bass trombone, the Appalachian mountain dulcimer and the Swedish bumblebee dulcimer (hummel). His work has been (or will be) published by numerous presses including *Dark Horses Magazine, The Button Eye Review, The Fairy Tale Magazine, Journ-E, The Red Ogre Review, Perennial Press, Lovecraftiana* and *Wingless Dreamer.*

Pete Barnstrom is an award-winning screenwriter and filmmaker whose projects have played at theaters and film festivals all over the world. He's shot documentaries in Greenland for the National Science Foundation, made movies with the Blair Witch guys (not that one), and seen one of his films screened at the Smithsonian. His experimental short films earned a grant from the Artist Foundation, and Amazon Studios bought a family film screenplay from him. He lives quietly in Texas and loudly elsewhere. You can find him on Twitter at @MistahPete and on Instagram at mistah.pete

Kim J Cowie lives in the UK and has been writing for many years. Kim has written several epic fantasy novels including *The Plain Girl's Earrings* and *The Witch's Box.* His short story *Eastern Vibes* has been published in the *Emanations Zen* anthology. He formerly worked in the electronics industry, and as a technical author.

Wayne Kyle Spitzer is an American writer, illustrator, and filmmaker. He is the author of countless books, stories and other works, including a film (*Shadows in the Garden*), a screenplay (*Algernon Blackwood's The Willows*), and a memoir (*X-Ray Rider*). His work has appeared in *MetaStellar—Speculative fiction and beyond, subTerrain Magazine: Strong Words for a Polite Nation* and *Columbia: The Magazine of Northwest History,* among others. He holds a Master of Fine Arts degree from Eastern Washington University, a B.A. from Gonzaga University, and an A.A.S. from Spokane Falls Community College. His recent fiction includes *The Man/Woman War* cycle of stories as well as the *Dinosaur Apocalypse Saga.* He lives with his sweetheart Ngoc Trinh Ho in the Spokane Valley.

Bridger Cummings resides in Aurora, CO, where he works as a writer and editor. He lived in Germany for six years before doing a world trip and returning to the states. He often has his head in the clouds when he isn't watching the sky with his telescope. www.bridgersmusings.com

Matthew Knight is an author of sword and sorcery and weird adventure fiction. Among various fantasy anthologies, his works have appeared in the recent DMR Books publications *Die by the Sword* and *Karnov: Phantom-Clad Rider of the Cosmic Ice.* He has upcoming stories slated to be printed in 2024 editions of

Cirsova magazine and *Tales from the Magician's Skull.* Matthew is the vocalist, guitarist, songwriter and lyricist of the epic heavy metal band *Eternal Winter* and the vocalist of *Cauldron Born* and *Noir Sensation.* He is also the co-founder of the group, *Haunted Abbey Mythos,* which has produced a theatrical, musical presentation of *The Beast of Averoigne* by Clark Ashton Smith. Matthew was recently nominated for two awards by the Robert E. Howard Foundation for a scholarly essay based on Howard's Solomon Kane tale, *The Hills of the Dead.*

Rick M. Clausen is a Bob Seger fan, and before he became a writer, he had a business career in International Marketing, where his B.S degree let him practice in the renowned Silicon Valley, and had the distinction of being included in Marquis Who's Who in America. He has authored and published four books; one a narrative of his time in the US Marines with his experiences in Vietnam, and the latest edition a collection of supernatural short stories titled *The Unnatural Order of Things.* His fictional stories of the supernatural have appeared in the publications of Hobb's End Press, in addition to online in *The Creativity Webzine.* He is a well-traveled strap-hanger, struggles to keep his score below a hundred on the golf course and lives in California.

Ethan Canter grew up in a log cabin his parents built in the secluded wilderness of Ontario, Canada. He studied writing on the west coast of Canada, and then completed an MA in creative writing at the University of Sussex, England. In 2014 Ethan moved to South Korea to work as an English teacher, but was forced to return to Canada in early 2020 due to the coronavirus pandemic. His existential horror story "The Briefcase" was published in *Everything Is So Political: A Collection of Short Fiction by Canadian Writers* (Fernwood Publishing: Canada, 2013).

Zackary Medlin is the author of the poetry collection *Beneath All Water* (forthcoming from Conduit Books). He holds an M.A./M.F.A. from the University of Alaska Fairbanks, a Ph.D. from the University of Utah, and now teaches writing at Fort Lewis College. He lives in Bayfield, CO, with his partner, their cat, and the hummingbirds, foxes, and mule deer that have graciously decided to share the yard with them.

Printed in Great Britain
by Amazon

42597190R00098